STRAY NARROW

Imogene Museum Mystery #7

D1522175

Jerusha Jones

CHAPTER 1

Frankie and I were agonizing over a seating chart. Normally such an administrative matter would've bored me to tears, and was much more suited to Frankie's particular degree of efficiency. But this once-in-a-lifetime assignment was crucial, and I couldn't keep my nose out of it.

Crucial to the future happiness of several potential couples we had our sights on. Not only were Valerie Brown and Mac MacDougal *finally* getting hitched, but their wedding reception in the grand ballroom of the Imogene Museum gave us an additional chance to play matchmakers.

"There," Frankie said with some satisfaction as she deftly swiped several strips of paper with names scrawled on them into new positions on the chart. "If we move Griffin Hughes over here, then we can squeeze Ralph Moses in beside Betty Jenkins."

"But what about Owen Hobart?" I objected. "That leaves him sitting at a table with a bunch of retirees."

"He's not dating anyone right now."

"Exactly."

Deputy Owen Hobart was young(ish), ruggedly handsome, popping with muscles, and painfully single. At least I thought he must be, although he'd never complained about his relationship status in my hearing. In truth, Owen had a tendency to not say much at all. But that didn't mean I couldn't make a few well-placed constructive assumptions. He needed a girlfriend.

The problem is, single and appropriately aged people of the female persuasion are hard to come by in Sockeye County. I blew my bangs out of my eyes.

"Val gave me this list of friends she thinks are coming." The Imogene Museum's gift shop manager and my favorite administerial maven sighed and drew the wrinkled page closer. "But we don't know them."

Worse than not setting Owen up at all?—setting him up with a painted, polished, ditzy city girl who didn't know a calf from a colt. Or a Colt from a Glock, if it came right down to it. Names penciled in Val's big loopy handwriting on a rumpled sheet of college-ruled notepaper were hardly inspiring.

"Ladies. Still plotting, I see." Rupert Hagg, director of the Imogene Museum and therefore my boss, world traveler, and inveterate flea-market haggler, leaned over the glass countertop in the gift shop and reviewed our strategy upside down.

Frankie nonchalantly curled her left hand around one corner of the chart as though she was protecting the loose strips from a stray breeze he might've brought with him through the museum's double glass doors. Wouldn't be unheard of—the Imogene is a leaky old girl. But I had to admire her tradecraft. Because Rupert was one half of one of the couples we were conspiring on behalf of, but he—so far—seemed blissfully unaware of those particular machinations.

Thankfully, his attention was snagged by Val's list. "Darcy O'Hare," he read from a line near the bottom. "Now there's a solid Irish name. I vote for her."

"As good as any," Frankie conceded. She slipped the page from his grasp and began snipping out the selected lady's name with a pair of ancient, industrial-strength shears.

Rupert swept off his tweed driving cap and wiped his bald forehead with the sleeve of his heavy peacoat. "All I can say is it's a good thing the two lovebirds decided to get married before your new exhibit goes on display, Meredith." He fumbled with unwinding a jaunty woolen muffler from around his neck. "Who wants to have their bridal-party photos taken next to scenes of horse thief hangings and moonshiners locked in stocks for public ridicule?" His whole body chuckled as he shook his head. "But if there are two people disinclined to be offended, I suspect they're Val and Mac."

Frankie giggled. "Mac's great granddaddy's in one of those photos. I do believe the legacy of spirits production and distribution is a matter of family pride."

"Besides," I added with a grin, quoting from the description I'd been working on to post beside the display, "it's reported that many of the townsfolk provided comfort and sustenance during his time in alfresco gaol. Earning brownie points with the most popular guy in the county, and quite possibly payback in kind at a later date. Prohibition was a losing battle from the beginning— certainly in the hearts and gullets of the local population."

Rupert's face was pink, and his bald pate glistened with a slight sheen of sweat. Not unusual, since his portly physique renders everyday activities like walking in from the parking lot somewhat exertive. But his eyes looked tired, the lids droopy, in spite of his crack about the county's illustrious distilling history.

"Are you getting sick?" I asked.

As if on cue, he doubled over in a debilitating sneeze, not all of which he caught on the other sleeve of his coat. "It's a possibility," he croaked, while grappling to unhook his coat buttons and finally fishing a large handkerchief out of his pants pocket.

"Go home," Frankie said authoritatively, forefinger extended with stern emphasis. "Now."

Rupert's watery gaze slid in my direction as he positioned the handkerchief for another hearty blow. As though he were asking permission. The man is a chronic workaholic. In a role he relishes like a hog in mud, but still...

I was already nodding along. "We have everything under control. Dennis confirmed the head count for the catered dinner. Jim Carter's handling the table and chair rentals. Val's mother is reportedly a dab hand at decorating within the constraints I outlined for her." I lifted my shoulders in a reassuring shrug. Since the museum is full of artifacts and displays of historical and artistic—if rather quirky—value, there's a long set of rules about where things like adhesive tape, thumbtacks, and hot glue can and cannot be placed. "We're good."

The reception wasn't being hosted at Mac's lubricating establishment, the Sidetrack Tavern, because Val had insisted he take at least one night off from slinging drinks and pay attention to her. Not that he needed prodding. He'd been tongue-draggingly enamored of her from the moment they'd met. And while potlucks are de rigueur for such festive occasions in Sockeye County, the weather and the sheer number of guests attending had

4

turned this particular event into a more formal affair out of necessity—and deemed the museum to be the best place to hold it. We'd proven—largely thanks to Frankie's administrative prowess—our ability to accommodate large groups in the past, and the rental fees always helped the museum's meager bottom line.

"What about the basement?" Rupert rasped. "Did you find those trunks I told you about?"

"Not yet." I lifted his red and white striped muffler from the counter and handed it back to him. "But there's still hope. I'm up to the First World War in my excavations." The museum's basement is a storehouse of jumbled collections, rejects, and plain old junk—and a liability disaster area which is why it isn't open to the public. Nothing down there is documented, but it's more or less layered by time period.

"I'm sorry you inherited decades of neglect when you accepted this job, my dear. But I'm nearly positive the coroner's tools—first Doc Halpern's and then Doc Merit's—are in a small, leather trunk somewhere in the dark recesses. I remember my father showing them to me when I was a kid. Doc Halpern was actually a veterinarian, but he was the most qualified citizen at the time." Rupert's chuckling turned into a phlegmy hacking fit as he reswathed his neck and head into a lumpy replication of a barbershop pole. "They'll make a nice addition to your exhibit because most of the deaths the good doctors confirmed in that era didn't occur peacefully."

Then he turned and, with a resigned wave over his shoulder, hunched back out into the gale-force wind and stinging ice particles that were currently registering as precipitation.

~oOo~

Thanks to her newly bolstered foundation and stone block construction, the Imogene is a bunker. Sorting over a century's worth of detritus in the basement is like tunneling in a mine shaft with all outside stimuli blocked. Except for the buzzing bank of overhead florescent lights, I was alone, digging in my own shadow, up to my knees and elbows in fossilized dust and grime.

And getting closer to the elusive coroner's medical kit, judging by the box of flapper regalia I'd just unearthed. It really was a useful exercise—this separating and collating of the reams of articles in the basement. Not one I had time for, truthfully, but still a thorough basement cleanout *was* a down-the-road looming task on my acres-long to-do list. Baby steps. I kept telling myself that projects seem less overwhelming when I can get at least a cursory grasp of the nature of the behemoth.

"Knock, knock," Sheriff Marge called from the bottom of the stairs.

"Over here," I hollered. "Behind the marquee with the semi-naked girl on it."

Her footsteps clunked on the concrete floor as she approached. "That's a doozy," she said, eyeing the massive painted sign propped against a couple old armoires—remnants of the Hagg family's vacation occupancy of the mansion a long time ago. "Is this something I should know about?" she asked, a stern officer-of-the-law frown on her face.

Sockeye County is pretty clean when it comes to skin shows and that type of thing, at least recently. It does have its Wild West past, however. Generally speaking, the current population's major vices are drinking, recreational marijuana, and a penchant for stupid risk taking at inopportune moments. (Note: There is a high correlation among these things.) And I'm pretty sure Sheriff Marge prefers it that way—in lieu of more serious problems.

I shook my head. "Before your time. This beauty was banned from Main Street by the all-female city council in 1925." I chuckled. "After gracing the facade of Lively's Pool Hall for all of three days. A marketing investment gone to waste, I guess. But Warren Lively should've known better. His third wife was on the council, and she was worried about one of the new girls supplanting her."

"*That* new girl?" Sheriff Marge jerked her chin toward the nearly pristine portrait of a buxom lass with pouty lips, clad in fishnet stockings and a feather boa and not much else.

"That was the rumor."

Sheriff Marge whistled softly. "Wouldn't want to be a fly on the wall in that household."

I pointed to a small scribble in one corner. "See the signature? This was painted by one of the premier pinup artists of the time. He'd later go on to become almost a household name during World War Two. The commission for this probably cost a fortune, and it has real historical value."

"You're not going to display it, are you?" Sheriff Marge snapped, clearly unimpressed by the marquee's provenance.

I propped my fists on my hips and grinned at her. "Prudence dictates otherwise."

She sniffed. "I should say so. I wouldn't want to have to deal with the phone calls from irate parents after the kindergarten class's annual museum tour."

"Most museums have a pretty voluminous stash of items they can't display for one reason or another. Sometimes the artifacts are too delicate and sometimes they're too risqué"—I pointed to the item in question—"or too macabre. Or too politically polarizing."

"Huh. Well, I'm adding to your woes, then." Sheriff Marge slowly creaked into a bent position and let the heavy box she'd had balanced on her jutted hip slide to the floor. "And that's not the last of it. I'll be tossing a box or two into the back of my Explorer every time I come out this way until I have the storeroom at the station cleaned out."

I already had the flaps open and was gently pawing through the items inside. "No problem," I replied eagerly—maybe a bit too eagerly.

Sheriff Marge's sigh was laden with weariness above me. I tipped my head back and studied her expression. She wasn't looking so hot, and I wondered if she was catching whatever viral bug Rupert had. But it was hard to tell in the harsh lighting. I also probably looked like an anemic ghoul who hadn't slept for forty-eight hours.

So it was better to just ask. "How are you?" Then I jumped up and dragged over a hideous ottoman upholstered in 1970's psychedelic velour. I patted the seat, resurrecting poofs of dust. "Take a load off."

Sometimes Sheriff Marge's leg aches. It's healed well after being broken in the collision that totaled her old rig and wiped out a tree, and she's back to stumping around with alacrity. She *never* complains, but sometimes I wonder if her body's just wearing down from all the years of playing mother hen to the entire county.

"Gonna act as shrink?" she grumbled, but complied.

"Tell me what this exhibit's about," I commanded. "Rupert thinks it's my idea, so we have success in that regard. But to accomplish your purpose, I'm going to need more information. You have a burr under your saddle, and it's been worrying you for a while."

"That obvious, huh?" She sighed again and mopped a hand over her face. "Petty crime's not petty when it's on a grand scale."

"Define *grand*."

"Well, yeah, it's relative," she admitted, shifting her weight and yanking one of the protuberances hanging from her duty belt out from under her left cheek. "But we're having a real rash of annoying incidents—broken windows in vehicles and businesses, thefts from farms and ranches, even from people's backyards, vandalism. It's not stupid teenager stuff, either. This seems to be with intent. I just can't figure out *what* intent. And it's keeping the deputies and me hopping."

"Hence clearing out space for a new hire?" I prodded. The sheriff's department was housed in a modular building up on blocks in the cracked parking lot of a former grocery store. The temporary-turned-permanent accommodations were neither glamorous nor spacious. But the county commissioners had just expanded Sheriff Marge's budget so she could hire another deputy, and that was cause for major celebrating.

But she wasn't rejoicing nearly enough. Her gray eyes remained somber in the garish light. "Not only that. Most people in this county aren't terribly subtle. But I'm just about at the end of my rope and am hoping that a prominently advertised exhibit about crime *and punishment*"—she raised her voice to a bellow to emphasize the words—"will put the concept at the forefront of their minds. And maybe act as a deterrent to the hooligans who seem to be running rampant lately."

"Do you mean this?" I asked, lifting a heavy metal object out of her box of grisly warnings. It was a massive animal trap, bigger than any I'd seen before—mastodon-sized—with angry teeth on the spring mechanism. Teeth that had a dried black flaky substance on them.

"Exactly. That was before my time too, but not by much. Haven't had a bank robbery since Copeland Smith got his leg stuck in that trap while he was hiding out up on Gifford Mountain with the loot. Poetic justice, I guess, since the trap was set by a poacher. He nearly died of septicemia before hunters found him, and did end up losing most of his leg to gangrene. Lot of good unearned riches do you when you have to use a wheelchair for the rest of your life."

"I can work with that," I said, nodding. "I suppose you wouldn't be surprised, but museum visitors do tend to gawk over the gory bits."

"Safe for kiddies, though," Sheriff Marge sighed, her strict-grandmother persona in full force.

"I'll put the exhibit on the second floor, with a warning sign about mature audiences only. The sad truth is, most kids see much worse on television today."

"They see worse than that, too," she replied, pointing toward the naked girl on the marquee. "I'm getting old."

"Aren't we all."

CHAPTER 2

Home. It was such a foreign concept. And a wonderful one. I was putting down roots with the man I loved. All because of the extreme generosity of a very dear set of elderly twins who'd retired and gifted us their old homestead, complete with campground, rickety farmhouse, ancient fruit trees, and a large charred spot where a barn used to be. All on the gorgeous bank of the Columbia River.

Every time I drove along the winding driveway, my blood pressure dropped ten points. And then I laughed aloud.

Because there was the sprightly female half of the pair of twins standing on the steps to the back porch with my ecstatic hound wriggling an enthusiastic figure eight around her legs.

"Harriet," I called, hopping out of my truck. "It's freezing out here. You could've let yourself in."

"Didn't want to intrude," she announced cheerfully, in absolute defiance of all her previous behavior. "Besides, Tuppence needed a rubdown. I thought your handsome husband would be here since the Army Corps of Engineers has all the locks closed for maintenance." She forced a mock frown underneath those bright blue eyes.

"He's pushing a dredge barge into position at the Port of Bingen today," I explained. "But he'll be home for

11

supper." One of the great joys of the limited traffic mobility on the Columbia River during the winter maintenance season was seeing a lot more of Pete. But I still couldn't possibly get enough of that man, and it seemed the condition might be contagious.

"Do you need something?" I asked, concern edging into my pleased surprise at Harriet's visit. The twins had been adjusting to their new environment at Edgewater Retirement Village reasonably well. For Herb, his day-to-day life was much quieter and less physically demanding—which he'd needed. But for Harriet, her social life had kicked up another few notches—also just the way she liked it, I'd assumed.

Tuppence was taking the opportunity to sniff my jeans legs for clues as to what I'd been doing all day, and I absently stretched down to tousle her ears while Harriet fidgeted, rubbing her colorful Fair Isle woolen mittens together in uncharacteristic reserve.

"Well, um, I was wondering…" she started, then quit sheepishly, looking like a lost little girl with a silvery ponytail poking out from beneath her fuzzy knit cap.

"Hmmm. Sounds like this is going to need a cup of coffee behind it." I tipped my head toward the door with an encouraging grin. "Come inside."

"That's just it," Harriet muttered as we stamped our feet on the worn floorboards of the porch and shed our outermost layers.

I flicked on the light switch inside the kitchen and made a beeline for the sink and Harriet's old-fashioned percolator coffee pot.

"I've turned into a wishy-washy giver," she continued, standing next to the large farm table and gazing about.

Along with the house and property, the Tinsley twins had also given us the vast majority of the house's contents. Pete and I hadn't only moved into a furnished home, we'd moved in amongst several generations' worth of accumulation. It was, frankly, like living in a working museum. And I didn't mind one bit. Why wouldn't I want to merge my personal and professional lives since I loved them both so much?

But I'd made a few changes, and Harriet seemed to be assessing them—with an expression of timid nostalgia on her face—so very unlike her usual pert and frank curiosity. My stomach knotted a bit on her behalf. How uncomfortable it must be to see someone else come in and modify the setting that had encompassed your whole life. The Tinsley twins had been born in this house.

I tapped the back of one of the chairs ringing the table. "Want to sit?" I asked softly.

But Harriet shook her head briskly. "No. I just want to get my rude request over with. Will you give me back my can opener? Please?"

I nearly burst out laughing. But managed to bite it back in the nick of time. Oh, for goodness' sake. "Yes. Yes, of course. Um, what does it look like?"

While Harriet was still mentally sharp—regularly fleecing her new friends at pinochle, according to the latest report from Sally Levine, the pastor's wife who'd been around to visit and was privy to such information—I'd found distinct signs of clever coping mechanisms for a mild degree of memory loss, particularly in the kitchen. This generally involved duplicates. There'd been no fewer than four can openers in various drawers, plus another one hanging from a hook next to the refrigerator. Seven Bundt cake pans, fourteen packages of muffin papers, three rolling pins, about thirty million washed and stacked plastic margarine tubs. You get the idea, and I'd only scratched the surface.

So I was at a bit of a loss to know *which* can opener she meant. It didn't matter. They were her can openers, and she could have them all. Except I suspected she might be embarrassed to find out she'd had so many.

"Herb and I enjoy the occasional can of soup when we don't feel like traipsing all the way down to the dining room for lunch," Harriet continued explaining. "The opener is old, a bit rusty, but it has that ergonomic handle. I paid eight dollars for it," she added hesitantly.

An exorbitant amount, indeed. And I knew exactly which one she meant. I'd been using it exclusively since Pete and I had moved in—precisely because of that lovely ergonomic handle.

I pulled open the drawer where I'd consolidated the most-used kitchen gadgets and handed the desired item to her with a flourish. "You certainly have good taste."

Harriet burst into tinkly laughter and dropped into the seat she'd refused earlier, hurdle apparently cleared. "You have no idea how much I've missed this thing. Crazy, isn't it?"

"Nope. Practical." I poured coffee into mugs and joined her at the table. "Are you missing anything else?"

Harriet blew across her mug, her gaze turning thoughtful. "Not really. I never really planned to be old, you know? I guess I thought I'd die out in the orchard by falling off a ladder at ninety-something the way my mother did. But this move to the retirement center gave Herb and me something to look forward to. Like a new adventure. Like summer camp."

"Are you sure?" I whispered. "It's a rather permanent form of camp."

"Oh, I'm sure." Harriet flapped her hand. "The heating system in the advanced care building has been acting up. Herb's been lending the custodian a hand in getting that balky thing up and running again."

Of course he was. But I appreciated what Harriet was telling me under the surface. As long as Herb was useful, he was happy. And as long as Harriet was surrounded by friends, she'd be happy too.

Tuppence scraped her nails on the kitchen door and whined. I scowled at her.

She has nearly impeccable manners, and intentionally scratching painted woodwork isn't in her usual repertoire. Not that the farmhouse wasn't worn, but still.

"Tupp!" I said sharply.

She cast a worried glance over her shoulder and wedged her nose against the crack between the door and the frame, her back end wiggling.

"She was a little preoccupied when Myrna dropped me off," Harriet said. "I just spotted the white tip of her tail in the tall grass next to your new pole barn, but she came when I called."

Tuppence *is* a hound, and she does follow her nose—sometimes to the blissful oblivion of all else. Except treats. Which Harriet is known for.

"Probably found a gopher," I muttered, "or a nest of field mice." Even though I didn't quite believe the excuse myself. "I think we displaced quite a few little creatures when we had the concrete slab for the barn poured." But Harriet and I were still studying my dog's back end while she made engrossed snorty noises into the crack.

When I glanced back at Harriet, she quirked a brow at me, and I nodded. Tuppence isn't usually given to false alarms, either.

"Got your slingshot?" Harriet asked, already rising from her chair.

"I'll leave it in your capable hands," I replied, retrieving the aforementioned item from an old wall-mounted mailbox on the way out and passing it off to her. "You know my aim's terrible."

"Not for lack of good instruction." She had a point. But I'd been remiss in practicing—what with being newly married and all.

Harriet and I reversed the process of warm layers and trudged down the porch steps. Tuppence was off like a shot, heading directly for the new barn. An arsonist had torched the Tinsleys' old barn, and I could almost feel Harriet tense beside me as we loped through the wet grass.

"It can't be anything too serious," I panted. "That's over and done with. Maybe a skunk."

In spite of being eighty-one years old and trotting along at a good clip, Harriet had the breath to argue with me. "Tuppence is a smart dog. She knows the difference. Has Sheriff Marge talked to you? There's been a rash of vandalism and thefts lately."

That put a kick in my step. Pete had been working hard on finishing the interior of the barn after our friends and neighbors had helped us raise the walls and roof in record time—before the winter rains set in. If anyone trashed the fruits of his diligent work, I'd personally pound them to a pulp.

But Tuppence's interest wasn't in the barn. She rounded the corner, and I lost sight of her. The only thing behind the barn, besides a mighty rushing river, several acres of unmown grass and some trees, was the fifth-wheel trailer I'd lived in before Pete and I had married, before we'd moved into a ready-made home.

By the time Harriet and I arrived, wheezing, at the trailer, Tuppence had set up camp at the base of the steps leading up to the door. And I didn't think it was from nostalgia. She enjoyed the far less cramped style of farmhouse living as much as I did. Her tail was swaying with tentative friendliness, her gaze focused, her whiskers working overtime.

"Looks like you have a squatter. I'll cover you," Harriet hissed. She crouched and anchored her elbows on her knees, forming a sturdy base for the slingshot she held at the ready. Somewhere along the way, she'd picked up a small stone, which she had pinched in the pouch. A fierce little white-haired Amazon warrior—that's my former landlady and benefactor.

Which would've been funny under other circumstances, since I would completely fill the doorway once I'd climbed the steps. Cover what, exactly? My backside?

I wondered if I should knock on the door to my own trailer and perhaps roust out the uninvited inhabitant. Or try stealth? It was a tossup, so I went for nonchalance and clumped up the steps and flung open the door.

To a dim and chilly interior that didn't appear to have changed since the last time I'd come out to retrieve a roll of parchment paper. It's weird the things you think you don't need and then, suddenly, do. But a quick foray in the trailer had beat a mad restocking dash to Junction General in the heat of a cookie-baking moment.

Tuppence was hard on my heels, and she wedged past my legs, her tail swishing madly. I took that as an excellent sign and followed her as she immediately banked to the right and climbed the few more steps to the bedroom portion of the trailer.

And there, in the middle of the queen-size bed, was a huddled lump.

CHAPTER 3

A huddled lump with rat's-nest hair, a dirt-streaked face, and the biggest, scaredest eyes I'd ever seen.

"She doesn't bite." The words flew out of my mouth before I even considered them, as Tuppence launched into an invasive bout of sniffing, poking her nose into all the folds and crannies of the duvet the child had heaped over himself. If it was possible, her tail was swishing even more violently now, in mad clockwise circles.

At least, I thought it was a boy. But the hair was long and shaggy and utterly unstyled, except by dirt and sweat and, most likely, rain squalls.

"Well, I never," said Harriet from close behind me, all promises of *covering* forgotten. "A stray."

"Tuppence winkles them out like nobody's business." It wasn't the first time she'd latched onto a creature in need.

Then it dawned on me that the object of our brief discussion was trembling, the soft mound of downy warmth vibrating slightly. I dropped into a squat to be closer to his level.

"My name's Meredith, and I live in that farmhouse." I made a pointing gesture in the right direction. "Are you alone?"

More soulful, fearful staring.

"Are you hungry?" Always a good bet.

The question struck a chord—I could see it in the shift of his gaze, just a flicker really. But he still didn't answer, not even with a dip of his chin. I'd cleaned all the perishables out of the trailer months ago, so there'd been nothing edible for him to forage.

By now, Tuppence had clambered up on the bed. She and her muddy feet aren't allowed on furniture, but this wasn't the time for a reprimand. Her hot, inquisitive breath in the boy's ear made him flinch, and he hunkered down deeper into the protection of the padded duvet as though it was a cocoon.

"Grilled cheese sandwiches," I offered. They're kid food, right? And also my own staple in the comfort food department, particularly when pressed for time and the refrigerator's nearly empty. "I could probably rustle up some cookies too. Something hot to drink?"

"Peach pie," Harriet added. She elbowed me. "I left several in the freezer, unless you've eaten them already?"

See what I mean about the amazing inheritance?

But the tag-team shtick was working. The boy's shoulders lost a bit of their tension. His gaze was moving now, bouncing from Harriet to me to Tuppence and back.

Tuppence sealed the deal by flopping on her side next to him and resting her head on the duvet over his knee. She emitted a gigantic, tongue-curling yawn as if this whole episode was just par for her doggy course— mission accomplished and time for a nap.

See? No threat.

Except tires crunched on the gravel drive outside, and the boy immediately tucked deeper into a protective curl. From what little I could see, he was painfully skinny under there.

"Myrna," Harriet breathed. "Fetching me. As much as I hate to leave this party, I'd better go." She grasped my forearm and tugged me down to whisper in my ear. "This one"—she tipped her head toward the huddled figure on the bed—"seems to need privacy. And you know how Myrna likes to talk," said one of the most thoroughly informed residents of Sockeye County. One of the main distributors on the rumor chain.

But she was right. As a talker, Myrna Bodwich just might trump all among very heavy competition.

"You'll need to put in an appearance, or she'll come looking for you. You know how it is," Harriet continued.

Indeed, I did. As the newest newlyweds in Sockeye County, Pete and I had had no shortage of drop-in visitors. Everyone seemed to take a vested—and persistent—interest in how we were getting on. Privacy had definitely been in short supply.

I laid a hand on the duvet over where I thought the boy's shoulder was. "Tuppence will keep you company. She's an excellent guard dog," I fudged. "You don't have anything to be afraid of. I'll be back in a few minutes." Then I scooted out of the trailer after Harriet.

~oOo~

Pete and I were soon to be supplanted in the newlywed department by Mac and Val. Hallelujah. Frankly, the day could not come soon enough as far as I was concerned.

But I responded to Myrna's well-intentioned quizzing as best I could under the circumstances. For some reason, the matrons of Sockeye County assumed that once a woman was married, she was suddenly starved for the detailed instructions of fourth-generation family recipes.

Secret recipes? Oh, no. They're open for dissection by all and sundry. Myrna spent ten minutes on the precise steps one must follow in order to faithfully reproduce her infamous caper-dill salmon-radish mousse canapés, starting with sending one's husband out to catch the fish before marinating it in brine and then smoking it. My eyes may have crossed at some point during the narrative. It was a far cry from a grilled cheese sandwich.

But I bundled my two friends off, satisfied that they'd done their duty by me. Harriet gave me a knowing squint over the top of the open car door as she climbed inside, and I knew I was on the hook to let her know how things progressed with our stray.

Then I placed a quick phone call and returned to the trailer to hone my persuasive skills. Or to drag the kid bodily into the warm farmhouse. He was a scrawny thing, and I was thinking that if I scooped him up, duvet and all, he wouldn't be able to claw his way out before I had him deposited in a far more accommodating—and nourishing—place. If only Tuppence could open the intervening doors for me.

~oOo~

Pete strode through the door at ten minutes after six—exactly on time. And engulfed me in a bear hug, all chilly dampness and stiff leather from the short ride on his Harley from the port where his tugboat, the *Surely*, is docked.

His lips, however, were searingly insistent. Pete kisses with a focused intensity that makes me weak-kneed. There is nothing wishy-washy about Pete's kisses. Or Pete's anything, for that matter. I was, indeed, a very happy woman.

But, a happy woman with a problem.

"Are we being watched?" he murmured, his stubble rasping on my neck.

I'm a sucker for blue eyes. Sapphire blue, specifically. With crinkles at the corners. I got a full dose of them when Pete pulled back a few inches and fixed me with a quizzical stare. Then darted his gaze to the left where two other sets of eyes returned the favor.

One pair of placid brown eyes—Tuppence is accustomed to Pete's and my shenanigans about the house and is routinely unimpressed. But Burke's wide eyes were more like a keen version of the Mediterranean on a sunny day with that greenish underhue that makes you think of mineral deposits. And they missed nothing.

"Yes, we're in the presence of a juvenile," I whispered. "Careful where you put your hands."

Pete grunted and squeezed me tighter, but those strong hands stayed safely pressed into my back.

Louder, I said, "This is Burke. He's been bunking in the fifth-wheel trailer for a couple days."

The greasy crumbs from two grilled cheese sandwiches were scattered over the empty plate and tabletop in front of him. Apparently leaving the boy alone for those few minutes, while I'd seen Myrna and Harriet off, had provided the emotional space he'd required to consider the compelling needs of his stomach. He'd said very little—other than his first name when I'd pressed the issue—but he'd meekly accompanied me into the house.

Tuppence had trotted at his heels the whole way and not left his side since. And it wasn't because he'd shared his snack with her—he'd gobbled both sandwiches all by himself, and in record time.

"That right?" Pete disengaged from me and shucked off his coat. "Well, I hope you like chili, Burke, because it's smelling good in here."

Have I mentioned that I love my husband? He didn't bat an eye, didn't object to having a stranger in his house, didn't make the kid uncomfortable with questions. Just took his presence for granted and pulled out a chair for himself at the table.

Tuppence scooted over to get her welcome-home ear scratching from Pete while I pulled the cornbread out of the oven and ladled up big bowls of chili from the Crock Pot.

We were saving the urgent questions for the person most qualified to ask them. The person I'd called earlier. Her knock sounded two seconds later, and she wasted no time in letting herself in, stamping her feet as though to leave the accompanying cold draft out on the porch.

My eyeballs just about popped out of my head, and I juggled a bowl of chili for a moment before relaying it safely to the table. In the first time in—well, in *forever*— Sheriff Marge was out of uniform.

In jeans and loafers. Loafers! With socks, of course, considering the temperature outside.

"You can scrape your jaw off the floor," she muttered as she shrugged out of her parka, revealing a floral print blouse tucked under a nifty hunter-green cardigan. A cardigan!

She looked like a Land's End catalog model. Well, except her stout, compact physique wasn't exactly catwalk material. And her short, tufty, salt-and-pepper hair was in need of a combing, and her reading glasses were riding low on the end of her nose. At least those aspects of her appearance were normal.

Her hat! It suddenly dawned on me. That iconic feature of her regular ensemble was nowhere to be seen. What's a sheriff without a Stratton hat?

A grandmother. That's exactly what she looked like. And what she really is, in her personal life. And maybe, just maybe, that's how she wanted Burke to view her, so he wouldn't be intimidated by the khaki creases and the badge and the duty belt and the gun and the Taser and the radio clipped to her shoulder, as she was—almost perpetually—attired.

I finally found my voice. "Sour cream? Honey butter?"

Pete gave me a nod, his eyes twinkling madly but remaining characteristically silent. We were going to pretend this was normal, even though Sheriff Marge had just shocked our socks off. All for the sake of a lost boy.

CHAPTER 4

Sheriff Marge waited until the boy was slathering his second wedge of cornbread with honey butter and I'd refilled his bowl. He had hollow legs, surely.

"Now, Burke," she said, "do I know your mother?"

How's a kid supposed to answer that? But Burke shrugged and shook his head. "She's dead," he mumbled around a mouthful.

There you go. Simple.

"How about your dad?" Sheriff Marge patted her left chest, realized her notebook wasn't in its customary pocket location, and returned to spinning her coffee mug in careful circles.

"Gone."

She inched forward to the edge of her seat. A parentless child was a very serious incident in Sheriff Marge's domain. "When did he leave?"

"August 23rd."

My brows mirrored Sheriff Marge's as they arched above her reading glasses. Nearly five months ago. And the boy was so precise in his answer.

"Have you been staying with relatives?" she asked in a softer tone.

But Burke shook his shaggy head again, seemingly oblivious to the concerned glances the adults were sharing across the table. "I can take care of myself. My dad taught me how."

None of us completely believed that grandiose claim as we watched him wolf down the last of the cornbread and lick his sticky fingers. A kid this hungry and scraggly wasn't being cared for by anyone.

But he did still have body and soul together five months later, if he was telling the truth. And that really was something.

Sheriff Marge rocked a little on her seat as though she was trying to find a level spot. Maybe because she was accustomed to sitting on all those lumps and bumps associated with her uniform. She wouldn't know cushy if it hit her in the backside.

"Where'd he go?" Sheriff Marge asked.

I got up and pulled a scratch pad and pencil from the junk drawer nearest the door, hoping to relieve some of Sheriff Marge's fidgety discomfort. She shot me a grateful glance as I slid them next to her elbow.

"Oil fields. Looking for work. Nothing around here," the boy said with a shrug.

Meaning jobs? That was most likely true. Sockeye County wasn't exactly a hotbed of ready employment. Or meaning oil? Then even more true. Nary a drop unless you counted what was in the barges and rail cars chugging their way down the Columbia River Gorge from their sources deeper in the interior.

"Bakken?" Sheriff Marge queried.

Burke shrugged again, surveying the dregs of our meal on the tabletop as though immensely disappointed.

I rose and snatched the cookie jar he'd dipped into earlier off the counter—and plunked it in front of him. There was no point in going through the niceties of arranging the cookies on a plate. All the better to keep him occupied so he'd continue answering Sheriff Marge's questions.

"Or maybe Alberta," he said, displaying a mouthful of partially masticated oats. Clearly, table manners hadn't been on the syllabus of survival techniques passed from father to son.

"You hear from him since he left?" Sheriff Marge continued prodding.

"Don't have a phone." Burke shook his hair out of his eyes and angled his arm inside the jar for another cookie.

"Where did you live with your dad?"

Burke stopped chewing for a moment, his lean face tight as he picked at a dried cranberry embedded in the new cookie. "Up on Gifford Mountain. Got a cabin up there," he mumbled. The suspect cranberry proved not to be a deterrent, and he crammed the whole thing in his mouth.

It was the second time that day I'd heard the name of that particular mountain. I'm still relatively new to the area, and there are a lot of mountains, hills, ridges, valleys, gulches, waterfalls, lakes, etcetera. Most seem to be named for some pioneering explorer who stuck it out the longest in a particular spot. I had some difficulty in telling one of the many layered greenish-to-bluish bumps on the horizon from another and no idea exactly where Gifford Mountain was.

Some distance, gauging from Sheriff Marge's reaction. The brows shot up again behind the reading glasses. "So what are your plans?" she asked.

As though Burke was an adult with full agency. My head swiveled back to view the small boy with his arm buried to the elbow in the cookie jar.

Those scrawny little shoulders shrugged again under the ratty T-shirt. "Hop a rail," he said matter-of-factly. But then he winced, ever so slightly, and those mesmerizing blue-green eyes shifted around our ring of concerned faces. "There hasn't been much in the traps lately. Figured my dad must have some money by now. I'll find him."

"I can do you one better," Sheriff Marge announced after a hefty sigh. She patted her left chest again, then ran her hands up and down her thighs under the table. I suspected she was feeling rather naked without all the accoutrements of her profession attached to her person. And she is, after all, a woman of action.

"You tell me his name, and I'll make some calls, see if we can locate him. Pete and Meredith here will put you up for a few days until I get the goods. Fair?"

I was staring at her like she must be daft.

But Burke was staring into the empty cookie jar. "Okay," he mumbled, his disappointed voice bouncing forlornly off the glazed ceramic surface.

~oOo~

The cook doesn't clean. It's a principle Pete had insisted upon and faithfully abided by in our new domestic arrangements. Unless he was the cook. Then he held a double standard. Have I mentioned lately that I'm spoiled?

He'd stacked the dirty dishes, scooped them into Burke's arms, and pointed the boy toward the sink. Apparently our guest was going to be doing a little work for his room and board, and I suspected a healthy education in soap and water and scrub brushes was occurring in my warm kitchen.

While I shivered out on the porch, the kitchen door shut firmly behind me. "What was *that*?" I hissed.

"Most of Gifford Mountain is government land," Sheriff Marge replied, huffing as she zipped her parka to her chin. "If they have a cabin up there, it isn't sanctioned with building permits or a property deed. Off-gridders, most likely, hoping no one would notice them, barely existing. People who want to live that far out usually come with massive chips on their shoulders, too."

So far, her explanation wasn't helping. I hugged myself tighter and ground my teeth together to keep them from chattering. A cacophony of clinking sounds tinkled on the metal overhanging porch roof. Not plopping, not splattering. Clinking. The percussive music would've produced a merry ambiance under other circumstances, but there were tiny frozen shards of ice in that rain.

"Which means I expect Burke's dad to be in the system," Sheriff Marge continued. "There'll be something—a drunk and disorderly, a disturbing the peace, maybe a misdemeanor theft or trespassing. Something. I'll put in some requests in North Dakota and points along the way, see if we get any hits."

"Surely you can't send the boy off to live with a father who neglects him so terribly? He's practically starving."

"No," she sighed. "But I don't want him disappearing again. If I can find the father, demonstrate that he's not fit to care for Burke, then we can move to the next step." Her steely gray eyes peered at me from under the brim of her fur-rimmed hood. "Maybe he'll learn to like living here, and we can convince him to stay. You and Pete would make terrific foster parents."

By the time I'd found my voice, she was off the steps and trotting toward her SUV with the sheriff's logo emblazoned on the side.

~oOo~

What do you do with a stray boy who might disappear again of his own accord, who has no money, no means of support, and an unfounded sense of self-sufficiency? Pete and I decided that I would take him to work with me.

Pete couldn't have Burke on a working tug. The kid's physical safety amongst the machinery was the primary reason. Pete's liability insurance would certainly rule out carrying such a young passenger. We also didn't know if Burke could swim, not that swimming ability would make much difference if a scrawny child fell into the churning Columbia in January. He'd be gone in an instant, life jacket or not.

The Imogene Museum had the predominant benefit of being on dry land. Well, *dry* was a relative term, but the old girl was a substantial fortress against the howling wind and clattering mixture of sleet, freezing rain, and plain old rain we were being plastered with.

And boring, I feared, for an eleven-year-old accustomed to roughing it. Her dusty halls and echoing rooms held a lot of enticement for me, but I could hardly expect my enthusiasm would rub off on the youngster.

I still found it difficult to believe Burke's claim that he was eleven. If it was true, he was hiding it well in a body more the size of a malnourished eight-year-old. Then again, as far as Sheriff Marge or Pete or I could tell, he hadn't lied about anything. And if I kept him close throughout the day, maybe he'd inadvertently reveal more about his past in a way that might help us secure his future.

So he was perched on my pickup's bench seat, way at the other end against the passenger door, all awkwardly angled skinny limbs and a blank expression of pure disinterest on his scrubbed face.

Because there had been some bathtub time the night before as well. Pete had ordered it, in a tone and with a manner I'd never witnessed from him before. And Burke had complied, without complaint or objection, splashing sedately behind the closed bathroom door for a good twenty minutes before emerging in a state that pretty much passed my inspection.

The whole dynamic between Pete and Burke was magic, and my estimation of Pete went up even more, if that was possible. I thought maybe Burke had been missing the considered guidance that is so aptly supplied by a responsible and measured adult male. Of course, Pete had been in the Navy, and perhaps he was accustomed to giving orders. Not to me—I'd never felt that way, but...new facets. Hmmm.

"So, we're sorting in the basement today," I finished explaining, glancing again at the melancholic boy beside me as the windshield wipers squeaked across the glass.

And then I remembered the pinup girl in the basement. The really provocative, intricately alluring pinup girl in fishnet stockings and feather boa. And I gulped, suddenly empathizing madly with Sheriff Marge's earlier objections. Try explaining *that* to an eleven-year-old boy. Rats. Rats. Rats.

I didn't know how long ago Burke's mother had died, but even if he'd been raised with females around, it was unlikely he'd ever seen that particular degree of femaleness in a normal, propriety-observing household. Not that he'd had that either, necessarily. But still...

Jim Carter was my saving grace. He had his pickup and trailer backed up over the curb and sidewalk to within inches of the double glass doors of the Imogene's entrance. Frankie had propped the doors open for him, and he was busy unloading stacks of folding chairs with a hand truck.

After I parked, and we'd hopped out of my truck, I plagiarized from Pete's playbook and suggested that Burke could help Mr. Carter with the very manly activity of heavy lifting. And Jim took it in stride, jutting his chin toward the open door to his pickup's cab. "Grab those rags, will you? We're going to have to wipe these chairs down once we get them inside. Dripping all over the parquet," he grumbled.

Burke scrambled to comply, and I stood there in awe, in the pouring rain. Why was it so easy? The kid was eager to please. And God bless crotchety Jim Carter. But was it *too* easy?

Frankie appeared at my elbow with an arm draped ineffectually over her helmet hair, trying to protect it from the onslaught of frigid moisture. "I'd ask if he's your nephew, but I know he's not." Her perfectly sculpted brows were riding high on her forehead.

"I'll explain," I whispered back, "but first things first…" I held up an apologetic finger as we hurried around the trailer's ramp. "Give me ten? And keep the boy up here until I get back?" I made a beeline for the stairs to the basement, my shoes squelching on the glossy oak parquet floor Jim was so gruffly concerned about.

Once I had the revealing marquee draped with two old painter's canvas cloths and a moth-eaten rug, I trotted back up the stairs and followed the wet tracks to a back hallway that was stacked to the gills with a few hundred folding chairs.

"This will be out of the way," Frankie burbled, clipboard propped against her hip. "We can cordon off this section, and visitors can still access the taxidermy room if they go around through the Victorian costume display first."

"You're the woman with the plan," I agreed.

"Got another two loads to get the rest of the tables in," Jim grunted, and checked his watch. "We'll be pushing it." He clumped off at an urgent pace toward the ballroom and his empty trailer beyond.

The goal was to have all the unloading completed before the museum opened at ten a.m. and Frankie was chewing her lip while squinting at the diagram with squiggles on her clipboard.

I patted her shoulder. "How much do you want to bet we have no more than a dozen visitors today, and none of them show up until after lunch? It's January, and it's raining," I reminded her, trying to be reassuring.

"I know." She blew out a deep breath and turned her attention to the small boy who was shuffling awkwardly from foot to foot. "Who's this?"

I figured an eleven-year-old could speak for himself. But it seemed two steady gazes on him were too heavy for his thin neck. His head dipped, and he stubbed his toe against the pile of rags waiting expectantly to be put to use.

"Burke Brightbill, ma'am," he said softly.

"Burke," she repeated. "Is that like *James Lee* Burke?"

A tentative smile appeared on his face, and he glanced at her from under his lashes. His sudden shyness was just about killing me. "Might be. My dad has read a bunch of those."

"Me too," announced Frankie, inexplicably surprising me yet again. But I shouldn't have been. I knew from experience that she was certainly one for adventure—both the fictional and real-life varieties, apparently.

"Well now, Burke," said Frankie, taking charge. "Once you have this floor mopped up, I think I could rustle up some hot chocolate in our kitchen. Not the fancy stuff, just from a packet, but does that sound like a fair deal?"

"Yes, ma'am." Burke was already on his knees, swabbing the rags over the water-splattered floor.

I followed Frankie into her own personal domain—the gift shop that was located in what had been the mansion's ladies' cloakroom just off the front entrance.

She whirled around and flashed a tentative, quizzical smile at me. "So, is there some indiscretion in your past that I need to know about?" Uncertain merriment danced behind her light-brown eyes.

I chuckled. "Not that kind. Burke's not mine. Or Pete's," I added as an afterthought. But then I sobered, remembering Sheriff Marge's foster parenting poke—prod, nudge, direct order? It'd been much more than a suggestion, coming from her—one I wasn't prepared to think about at the moment.

So I quickly filled Frankie in on the excitement of the past afternoon and evening. Her brows rose in increasing increments and her mouth formed into a perfect *O* as I proceeded.

"That poor child," she murmured when I'd finished, shaking her shellacked hair.

"While it feels like child labor, I do think it'd be a good idea to keep him occupied today."

She was already nodding. "No reason he can't be part of things. I expect he'll appreciate feeling useful. We're *all* working." She glanced at her clipboard again, and I took that as a cue to get my own rear in gear.

CHAPTER 5

My office is cramped on a normal day. And this wasn't a normal day, even in my highly varied role as curator of an exceedingly eclectic collection of memorabilia, art, historical artifacts, and other assorted miscellanea. As a former nursery on the third floor, my office's overwhelmingly redeeming feature is a huge picture window that overlooks the Columbia River—essentially providing a front-row seat to the most breathtaking scenery on the planet.

But I might be biased.

Burke, however, seemed to agree with me. He shoved the leather case he'd been carrying onto my already crowded desk and went straight to the glass, leaning so close that his breath left splotches of condensation on the cold surface.

"It's like being in a tree house," he murmured.

Was that a clue? "Do you have a tree house?" I asked as softly as I could.

He shook his head without turning, still transfixed by the view. "No, but I've read about them."

It was his second mention of reading—either his or his father's. I'd highly suspected that Burke's schooling had been neglected, given the most recent living arrangements he'd disclosed. But if he could read, and enjoyed doing so, and had had access to books, then that changed a great deal about my perspective.

The second best feature of my office are the bookshelves that line the remaining walls. "You're welcome to read anything in here," I offered even though most of the tomes are specialized histories, geographical and topographical studies, records of archaeological digs, and in-depth exposés of very specialized art geared toward the rabid collector. "Since we found the coroner's medical kit so quickly, I'm afraid the rest of our day will be pretty quiet."

The more academic aspect of my job—research—is truly fascinating. To me. But from Burke's perspective, it would look a lot like me sitting in a chair, clicking through websites on my laptop and taking notes. In other words, boring.

"So you're going to build an exhibit?" Burke wandered over to lean against the edge of my desk, those blue-green eyes slowly—and thoroughly—raking the contents of my office.

I'd been stacking the boxes containing Sheriff Marge's contributions from the storage closet at the station in neat rows, and they took up most of the available floor space.

"That's right." I nodded, appreciating his use of the term *build*. It's like that, really. Taking all the pieces and constructing a cohesive exhibit that tells an engaging story. But I was worried that Sheriff Marge's exhibit might require more detailed information than I had access to.

The two cultural bastions of Sockeye County are the Imogene Museum and the tiny historical society that is manned by one headstrong and overbearing matron and the few acolytes she's managed to coerce into doing her will. Altogether, they have about three cardboard file boxes of old photographs, a few tattered Victorian hair wreaths, and some needlework accessories from pioneer women in their collection which they'd been trying for over a decade to set up in display cases in one of the minions' garages. Their whole situation was going nowhere fast.

Consequently, I tried to stay out of that mess and had instead made friends with the directors and principal volunteers who serve in the less contentious historical societies in all the counties surrounding my own. Just in case. Because sometimes stuff—actual physical items and, perhaps more importantly, lore—migrates. If I hit a dead end, I had people I could ask.

"Including that?" Burke pointed to the grisly bear trap that was poking out of the top box in the nearest stack.

"Yeah." I decided to test an idea. He was eleven, after all. "That trap stopped a bank robber. He got his leg stuck in it up on Gifford Mountain." I watched him closely out of the corner of my eye.

Burke snorted. "Traps all over the place up there. He should've watched where he was walking."

Okay, not the response I'd been expecting. I cocked my head and refrained from pointing out that the robber had been captured in the 1960s. Maybe trying to nudge Burke into revealing more about himself wasn't the best course. And maybe time stood still where he came from.

"How do you feel about arranging all that stuff into chronological order?" I asked. That likely wouldn't be the way I'd end up displaying any of the items from Sheriff Marge's collection. I had a feeling topical kiosks were going to be the best method, but I had to start somewhere, and cataloging all the bits and bobs of paper, reports, dry and crusty evidence, etcetera was still necessary.

"Sure." Burke shuffled forward and gingerly lifted the well-used bear trap from the box. Clearly it was already the pièce de résistance of the—as yet unformed—new exhibit.

In short order, it became obvious that Burke was quick, whip-smart, and highly intuitive. He watched every move I made and was mimicking them closely within a matter of minutes as we gently started distributing Sheriff Marge's items into piles based on decade.

I fetched a bunch of big plastic tubs to hold the three-dimensional items, and the papers were slotted into special archival boxes. We'd go back and do the fine-tuning by date later.

But the most fascinating—and disturbing—items were housed in evidence pouches. Some had tags with spidery, faded handwriting attached to them and some just had their identification information scrawled onto the outside of the pouch. Bullets, shell casings, a pair of scissors, knives with dried and cracked wooden handles, lots of scraps of clothing—much of it stained with various substances I didn't want to think about, a child's torn rag doll, a couple silver whiskey flasks that would still fetch a pretty penny, lengths of rope. And more—much more.

"They don't need these anymore?" Burke finally asked after a long bout of working silently but companionably.

I lifted my head to find him fingering an extremely rusty revolver that had a tag dangling from the trigger guard. My heart leaped into my throat, and a sharp warning nearly pushed its way past my lips. But then it died just as quickly, and I swallowed it down.

Because Burke *was* being careful. And I didn't want to sound like a worrisome nagger.

"Right," I said instead, attempting nonchalance. "In most cases, the crimes have been successfully prosecuted and the appeal process has been exhausted, so the sheriff's office isn't required to store the evidence anymore. In the other cases, the statute of limitations has run out, so the case *can't* be prosecuted. Sheriff Marge told me there are a few cold cases in here that she really wishes could've been solved, but the perpetrators would be long dead by now and beyond the reach of human justice. They'll likely remain a mystery." That was a lot of big words for a kid—on a topic that stymied most adults in the United States, but he absorbed them without apparent confusion.

Burke had a knack for picking out the items that would make the best displays. A few minutes later, he held up a packet of painfully obvious counterfeit bills. They appeared to have been hand drawn by a preschooler. *Dollars* was misspelled as *dollors* and Andrew Jackson sported what looked like a Mohawk hairdo—way, way before the style had been briefly trendy on old white people.

"Not too bright," I whispered.

Burke shook his head with a mischievous grin and went back to sorting.

In the late afternoon, we uncovered a reenactment diorama from the days long before PowerPoint and digital pictures. It almost looked like a dollhouse, but the scene inside was not exactly one of domestic bliss. Half spectacle for the jury and half forensic training tool, it was morbidly detailed with careful clothes sewn to the soft figures and matchstick furniture glued in place. There was even a replica murder weapon under the bed and several "bloody" footprints in what appeared to be red India ink.

"Pretty clear who did it, huh?" I muttered, rethinking, yet again, whether or not bringing Burke to the museum had been a great idea.

He seemed mature. He seemed small. He seemed eager to please, but he also seemed reserved. And now he seemed scared. I didn't know how it was possible, but those pristine mineral eyes got bigger and the edges of his lips turned white.

"Did he go to jail?" Burke's voice was small and scratchy. And incredibly vulnerable.

Remorse washed over me. What had I just dredged up from his past? Most people don't go out and live alone in the deep woods without some sort of horrible prompting. Made me wonder what Burke's father—or Burke himself—had encountered that turned conventional sociability into something to be shunned.

"I'm sure he did," I lied. The truth was, I wouldn't know until I'd read the case notes that went with the diorama. But with the depiction glaring us in the face, it seemed a good bet the jury had found a preponderance of evidence.

I pulled the diorama toward me and piled a few folders on top of it, effectively covering the worst of the scene.

~oOo~

While Burke was in the men's room washing a day's worth of ancient grime from his hands, I placed a quick call to Sheriff Marge.

"I got nothing," I said, "except that he's excellent company, highly intelligent, patient, a hard worker, and has had a reasonable level of education so far. Also, he's extremely hungry, but you know that bit. Tomorrow I'll have to pack three times as many snacks."

Sheriff Marge grunted. "Did he exhibit any particular fears—of men, loud noises, claustrophobia, that kind of thing? Any signs of abuse?"

"We didn't examine him," I stuttered, thinking of the bath Burke had administered to himself, privately, the evening before. "Should we have? I mean, I haven't seen any obvious bruises or anything, but not a lot of his skin is showing—you know, because it's cold out and he's wearing long sleeves and long pants." This was so beyond my normal realm of experience that I hated to think about all the possible ways of hurting a child. "He moves okay," I added quickly. "Not like he's in pain or has had any recently broken bones."

"That's all right. We'll give him a period of adjustment, see what he feels like sharing when the time is right. You're doing good," she added with an encouraging gruffness.

I wasn't so sure. I told her about finding the diorama and Burke's reaction to it.

Sheriff Marge grunted. "Forgot that was in there. But you can tell Burke that not only did Hugo Clayton go to prison for stabbing his mistress and her other lover to death, his trials went through without a hitch and he was rather expeditiously hanged out at the penitentiary in Walla Walla." She sighed heavily into the phone. "Or maybe you won't tell him all that. Been a while since I had boys his age under my roof. Working in the profession I do, you kind of just end up telling it like it is..."

"I understand," I said quickly. "Any word back on his father?"

"Still waiting to hear. Could be a while since we don't know exactly where he went or what route he took, or if he ever actually got to where he was going."

"Can you register him as a missing person?"

"Already have. But there's nothing to go on. No photo. No identification. Only Burke's word that his father's complete name is Cullen Brightbill and his approximate age. I'm also having a records check done with the state to see if we can find their birth certificates—both Cullen's and Burke's—but if they weren't born in Washington, then..."

Again, I could fill in the blank. The situation did seem hopeless.

Burke emerged from the restroom and halted skittishly about fifteen feet away, watching me with tentative curiosity and no small amount of hesitation.

"Catch up with you later," I said to Sheriff Marge by way of little-ears code, and plastered a cheerful—and hopefully reassuring—smile on my face as I hung up. I had a boy who needed his supper.

CHAPTER 6

Sheriff Marge's timing is impeccable. My phone rang just as I was licking off my fork after indulging in a headily delicious slice of Harriet's peach honey pie—the one that had been too frozen to eat for Burke's inaugural dinner the night before. It wasn't frozen now. It was warm and syrupy and perfect with vanilla ice cream melting down the sides of each slab.

Both Burke and Pete were working on their second slices. I had to rinse my hands at the sink so I wouldn't gum up the phone's keypad. Once I saw the caller ID, I ducked out onto the porch in case privacy was in order.

It was.

"Bad news," Sheriff Marge sighed. "I've gotten a report on Cullen Brightbill."

"Jail?" I whispered.

"That would be good news." Sheriff Marge's voice was heavy with weariness, and my stomach rolled into leaden knots at the finality of her words. "He's dead."

"Is there proof?" I gulped. "Could it be a case of mistaken identity?"

"Afraid not. I have his medical records and death certificate here on my desk. He told the nursing staff he had a boy named Burke. Repeated Burke's name with frantic urgency while he was delirious, to the point that they had to sedate him. He was in a severely weakened condition when they found him and brought him in, but it was pneumonia that got him."

Tears built up on the rims of my eyelids, but it was too cold for them to fall. I upended a split piece of firewood and sank down onto the precarious temporary seat, my goose-bumped arms crossed over my aching middle. "What happens to Burke now?"

"He's a ward of the state."

"I hate the sound of that."

"Me too. Which is why I've already made an executive decision. I wasn't kidding when I said you and Pete would make terrific foster parents."

"What have you done?" I whispered.

"I filed a sheriff's petition for protective custody and listed you two as his guardians—for now. That'll give Hester Maxwell down at Children's Services the chance to run you through the foster parent program and get you certified without disrupting Burke's location. If you're willing," she added softly. "He's already had a lot of upheaval in his young life, and he doesn't need any more tonight."

I was the most terrified and the most certain I'd ever been in my life, even more than in those few minutes before I'd said "I do" to Pete.

"Yes," I breathed. "We'll do it."

"Good," Sheriff Marge grunted. With some relief, I thought.

"You said *found*," I backtracked. "Cullen Brightbill didn't admit himself to the hospital?" I was going to have to find some way to explain this tragedy to his son, and I needed every single detail I could grab.

"He was living out of a car in a makeshift homeless camp on the edge of Sidney, Montana. Residents were complaining, so the Richland County sheriff's department cleared out the camp and found a few men in need of medical attention. Cullen Brightbill was one of them. It's been a rough winter out there. But his medical treatment is the one reason I was able to locate him so quickly. Sheriff Monroe is mired in overtime, but he gave me a courtesy call because the Brightbill name was familiar."

"I don't know where Richland County is," I murmured.

"Far eastern edge of Montana, right in the thick of the Bakken Formation. Lots of oil wells, but that doesn't necessarily mean there's enough work to go around."

"Did Cullen have any personal possessions, anything that Burke can remember him by?"

"Sheriff Monroe's packing up and sending the contents of the car to me. I told him to sell the car and use that money to help offset Brightbill's medical bills because that's all they're going to get from his estate. And Meredith," Sheriff Marge added, "a couple deputies and I will go look for the cabin on Gifford Mountain that Burke talked about. I don't like loose ends, so we'll board it up, pack any personal items in from there as well. We'll get him as much history as we can."

"Thank you." The tears were dropping now, straight onto my knees in frosty spludges.

~oOo~

We didn't tell Burke until the next morning. Mainly because I had to talk with Pete first. After all, I'd included him in a huge, life-changing commitment, and he had the right of first refusal. I also needed to be able to pass along the horrible news without bawling my own eyes out in front of the kid.

So I bawled on Pete's shoulder after we went to bed. I'm not quite sure how I kept it together in those intervening hours of routine washing up and tidying and preparation for the following day.

"Babe, babe, babe," Pete murmured into my hair, his arms warm and strong around me. "You did the right thing. Absolutely we will take care of Burke. No question."

I sniveled pitifully.

Pete pulled my left hand up to rest on his chest, and he began to massage the simple gold band around and around on my finger. It was his secret code to me—one he'd started on our wedding night—and I loved it. Just a subtle reminder that we were glued together for life now.

"I'll clear out the room at the end of the hall and bring in the appropriate furniture," he said, already moving on to practical matters. "Good thing Herb and Harriet left us so much to choose from." I nearly snickered through my tears—it was the understatement of the year. "We'll let Burke pick what color of paint he wants, yeah? Get him enrolled in school. As soon as he's ready," Pete added in his soft deep rumble as he tilted onto his side and propped his head up on the heel of his hand to look at me in the dark. "We won't push him."

I rolled my head from side to side on the pillow in agreement.

"He needs to continue going to the museum with you in the meantime. Provided Rupert's okay with that." Pete's thoughtful tone seemed to resonate in my chest. "Burke needs to see a normal, good life in operation before he'll be able to fully trust us. Babe, you're a master at that."

"Living a normal, good life?" I croaked.

"Yup. You're the bravest woman I know."

I released a watery chuckle. "Current evidence suggests otherwise."

"Temporary and passing, but that's why you have me." His words were muffled against my neck, and I took solace in his embrace.

~oOo~

That little pale face was killing me. So far, I'd managed not to shed a tear, but my eyes were brimming again, for about the hundredth time since Pete and I had somberly laid out the facts as we knew them at the breakfast table.

I decided more coffee was in order and quickly rose to lean over the sink and stare out the window at a frosted winter wonderland for a minute.

Burke looked even smaller than he had when huddled under the duvet in the trailer. A wisp of a boy who just might vanish altogether. Which was one of the main things I was worried about. That he'd flee—again—before his grief could settle into place.

What place that was, I didn't know. But in my experience, grief often feels like an anchor, and I was *hoping*—weird term, I know—that Burke's grief would somehow anchor him in Platts Landing, with Pete and me. Willingly, though—not under duress.

Burke hadn't cried either—or spoken. We were all valiantly dry-eyed. But he was absolutely stricken, sitting with his hands tucked under his thighs, the toes of his sneakers not quite dragging on the floor from the height of the chair seat, his pointed little chin just an inch above the tabletop.

I slid a fresh mug in front of Pete and cradled my own as I perched my fanny back on the warm seat I'd just left. It was disconcerting, that little surge of warmth, and I shifted on the hard surface.

Burke shuddered, deep and involuntary, the spasm racking his entire body. I took a chance and touched him for the first time since we'd broken the news, a soft hand on his shoulder. He flinched, but neither of us pulled away. He was so very skinny under the thin T-shirt and way-too-large wool sweater we'd scrounged for him.

"We'll go into the museum today," I said quietly. He'd enjoyed being in the museum the day before, and sticking to a routine seemed advisable—what little we could cobble together at the moment. "There's a lot of work to do," I added hopefully. I appreciate the chance to work when I'm in emotional distress, and I wondered if rigorous physical activity would have the same soothing effect on a child.

Burke just nodded mutely and kicked at the table leg. Pete rose to clear the dirty dishes and shared a glance with me, his expression strained and solemn, the lines around his gorgeous eyes etched deeply.

Tuppence was a last-minute addition to our party. She'd tagged along as Burke and I carried our insulated lunch bags out to the pickup, and when I opened the passenger door for Burke, she followed him right on up to the bench seat. He had to scoot over to make room for her since she always insists on riding shotgun and her gangly seventy pounds takes up a lot of space.

I shook my head, marveling at the intuition of dogs. Normally, I don't take Tuppence to work with me. Dogs in public institutions are generally taboo, and she usually enjoys the chance to wander the campground, sticking her nose into gopher holes and patrolling the perimeter. But today she clearly had an agenda. Besides, she's well-mannered around people and not too stinky.

Burke needed all the loving he could get, and if it happened to come with four legs and long floppy ears and mild halitosis, so much the better.

Frankie knew. I'd sent her a text so we wouldn't have to speak about the situation in front of Burke. I'd also texted Rupert, who had grudgingly admitted that he ought to remain quarantined at home since his virulent head cold had progressed to the messy, splattery stage. He gave me carte blanche with regard to Burke's presence in the museum, just as he did with everything else. Frankly, he was the most lenient boss in the world.

CHAPTER 7

The morning was full of more potential exhibit sorting, so we camped out in my office. Even within the confined space, Burke stuck to me like a tenacious shadow—helpful, somber, never making a fuss, but remaining steadfastly within arm's reach. I desperately wanted to pull him into a hug and squeeze him—to somehow force all the pain away. But he was as skittish as he was clingy, and I didn't want to thrust invasive physical contact on him without permission. We still didn't know what his background was, what his past contact with adults had been flavored with—goodness, kindness, or evil?

He missed his dad, though—there was no question about that.

Shortly before lunch, I attempted a commiserating form of therapy. At least, I hoped revealing my own past pain would be of help to Burke. "My dad's dead too," I mentioned as I tapped police reports into folders by date. We were sitting cross-legged on the floor, dusty artifacts piled around us in concentric circles. "He died when I was four. But he'd been gone for a while before that." I didn't see the need to euphemize for Burke, so I added, "From drugs. He overdosed."

Burke shnuffled—from dust or allergies or a blossoming head cold of his own or grief, I couldn't tell. "I kinda knew," he replied so quietly I barely heard him. "My dad wouldn't leave me for so long unless something bad had happened."

Factual acknowledgment. Was that progress along the grief spectrum? But I had to seize the opportunity while it was sitting there in the silence between us. "Had he left you alone before?" I asked in as gentle of a tone as I could muster.

Burke nodded. "We practiced a few times. He had to go out hunting anyway. So I held the fort, and marked the days off on the calendar for him." The tiniest flicker of a smile swept across his face before those huge, somber eyes regained dominance. "He said I was good at it."

I grinned back at him. "What does that mean, *holding the fort*? Sounds like you'd need a musket and a powder horn. Any Redcoats around?"

I'd been trying to lighten the tone just a bit, hoping to set him at ease—and to test his knowledge of American history at the same time, multitasking at its finest—but he answered with the utmost sincerity.

"Just drowsy black bears usually, and sometimes a cougar. The little creatures wouldn't stick around if they saw me, except this one big raccoon that I made friends with." Again, his face was brightening. "We had some honey in the cabin, and I'd smear a little on a stick. He'd lick it right off then wash his face over and over again like he had a germ phobia."

Chuckles. I could hardly believe my ears. The little guy beside me was chuckling jerkily in short hiccups, as though his skill in the expression of mirth was rusty and he didn't really know how to do it. I couldn't help but join in.

"I've never had that kind of encounter with a raccoon, but Tuppence here"—I pointed at the hound who'd wedged herself under my desk for lack of snoozing space anywhere else—"met a cranky skunk once. We both reeked for days after that."

Burke's face crinkled with distaste. "Oh yeah. I stay away from *them*," said the young voice of experience. "But if you shoot them right between the eyes, then you might not get any scent on you. You still have to be careful when you skin them, though."

That entire set of facts was news to me, and I squinted at Burke out of the corner of my eye, still keeping my hands busy with paper shuffling. It was difficult not imagining the recoil of a rifle slamming his frail body to the ground. Was he a marksman at the tender age of eleven? It wasn't unusual in these parts, actually, for kids to learn how to shoot—out of necessity, for self-protection in the woods, and often simply because the rest of their family members already knew how. Shooting in Sockeye County was kind of like riding a bike anywhere else. It was the odd person out—including me—who wasn't proficient in that basic life skill.

The afternoon was spent in preparation for the wedding reception. We trooped downstairs to help Frankie tackle the myriad tasks on her to-do list. And Frankie pressed Burke—sensitively and gently, in a way I hadn't yet—by sending him on errands throughout the museum, testing the strength of those tethers he'd seemed to be holding so closely.

He adapted immediately to her requests, darting into the Imogene's nooks and crannies to fetch things or count things or scout for and consolidate all the assorted accoutrements she needed, Tuppence hard on his heels with a degree of canine eagerness and tail jauntiness I hadn't seen from her in a long time. Frankie gave Burke a safety whistle from among the gift shop's various logo-ed trinkets in case he should get lost in the sprawling mansion. It's amazing what kinds of items can be custom screen-printed, and I was pretty sure Frankie had special-ordered all of them to round out the selection of enticing mementos in the shop.

The Imogene is a great labyrinth of public spaces and even more convoluted private back hallways and former servant stairwells, including, even, a multistory laundry chute that's equipped with climbing handholds and footholds for the more adventurous explorer. One of the great perks of having an experimental architect at the helm back in the day when building codes were far more lenient.

I hoped the mansion's idiosyncrasies would delight Burke, as they should any curious, energetic child—any normal child who wasn't grieving. It was what the Imogene had been built for—even though her original purpose hadn't been truly fulfilled—the housing of boisterous children and their extended family.

It's easy to forget the old girl had been a house—with all the usual trappings of high-class domestic life—before she became a cultural institution, but Frankie was taking full advantage of that fact, tapping into the Imogene's stores of vases, table linens, even some fancy silver serving pieces and candelabra, for the wedding reception. A wealth of riches.

Tired but uncomplaining, dirty with a degree of compacted grime that would require a long soak in the tub, and a stomach that had recently resumed growling audibly to remind everyone nearby of his nutritional needs, Burke was also obliging me by washing up in the men's room again, enabling me to sneak in another phone call to Sheriff Marge for my daily update.

"Sorry," she grunted, the regret and resignation deep but muffled in her sigh. "Had an emergency out on the far side of Lupine. Except it wasn't, but we didn't know that until the contractors showed up to resume work."

"Huh?" I said.

A car door slammed, and the sound quality of the call jumped up a significant notch. She must've just hoisted herself into the driver's seat of her snazzy new police command vehicle, shutting out the dull thumping cacophony that had been in the background. It had sounded like jackhammers. How well I knew that headache-inducing aural assault.

"It'd be funny, except it's not. Wasted an entire day." Sheriff Marge wheezed a bit—a sort of gruff air expulsion that I knew from experience was accompanied by a series of jiggling ripples that radiated out from her Kevlar-coated core. It made me grin, just thinking about it, and I felt tension I didn't know I'd stockpiled ease out of my own shoulders.

"Do you know Ira Cupples?" Sheriff Marge continued.

"The only Cupples I know is Bernice." I gritted my teeth against the memory of that overbearing harridan— the one I avoided assiduously, the one who appointed herself dictator of Sockeye County's woeful historical society and held the title with a tenacity and subtlety befitting Imelda Marcos.

"Her father-in-law." Sheriff Marge made the connection for me. "He lives with Bernice and Junior. Has dementia, which has been getting rapidly worse, apparently. About two months ago, I had to take away his driver's license. He told me in no uncertain terms what he thought of me for doing that. If I didn't know better I'd think Bernice was his blood relative instead of just married in. Those two have exactly the same temperament."

The idea of two such human scourges operating in my vicinity gave me shudders.

Sheriff Marge's voice returned to its usual weary gruffness. "But today he didn't recognize me. Still remembered how to dial 911 though. And how to wave a shotgun around. Didn't remember to put shells in it, but there was no way we could tell that from fifty yards away."

"Are you telling me you had a standoff with Mr. Cupples?" I asked quietly.

"Oh yeah," she sighed. "Full response. All my deputies and me, with three state troopers and about half of Klickitat County's deputies assisting. All for a nut case with a shotgun who forgot that his daughter-in-law was having some renovations done to their old shed. So she can finally display the—and I quote directly from her recent irate phone call—*priceless historical artifacts so indicative of our county's rich and varied history*."

I groaned straight into the phone. "Which means her minions finally told her to shove it, and she has to do her own hard work."

"I got no comment on that," Sheriff Marge stated wryly.

"I still don't really understand," I replied. "Mr. Cupples called you and then he wanted to take a potshot at you?"

"Pretty much. He was under the delusion the place had been robbed, due to the construction crew having moved junk out of the way in order to begin work. Frankly, there's nothing in that shed worth stealing, but any change seems to upset Ira. So he was out there defending a pile of trash from unknown thieves, and then he forgot how to tell the difference between cops and robbers when we arrived."

"How'd you, um, disarm him? I mean it's over, right?" My tongue stumbled over the scenario that was still disjointed in my imagination. If there was one job in Sockeye County I didn't want, it was Sheriff Marge's. "Peaceful resolution?"

"He fell asleep. Sat down on a bale of hay and slumped over to his left side. Initially we thought maybe he'd had a stroke. But nope. Just exhausted from all the excitement—excitement of his own creation, I should point out."

I had no words. Should I offer condolences? To whom? For what, exactly? My main thought was that I was glad I'd had no part in that situation. But then the door of the men's room swished open, and I remembered that I had a different problem on my hands—a little boy's broken heart.

"So that means you weren't able to pursue those leads you had in mind today?" I asked quietly as Burke shuffled up to me.

Sheriff Marge's tone immediately resumed officialdom. Somehow she knew I had an observer on my end. "Correct. Tomorrow, I promise. I'm going to tell the emergency dispatchers to double-filter any requests before they pass them through, and we'll all go out to Gifford Mountain. Dale's recruited a few old-timers who know the area well and are willing to help supplement our search party."

"Thank you," I whispered.

"We'll get some answers, Meredith," Sheriff Marge promised before she hung up.

CHAPTER 8

It was a sound I'd never heard before. My eyes flew open in the dark, and I held my breath, straining to hear a repeat of the soft whimper. Had I been dreaming?

Beside me, Pete was breathing evenly and deeply, one arm crooked under his head and the other slung across my belly—a warm and comforting weight.

We live out in the country, and there are all kinds of nocturnal noises, usually from rambling creatures foraging for food or fighting or mating. Sometimes it's hard to tell the difference between those activities just from the sounds the animals make. But this noise had come from inside the house, I was pretty sure.

But not sure enough to wake Pete—just yet.

The next time the whimper came, it extended into a short but muffled keening, high-pitched and young. Very young.

I sat bolt upright and swished my hand over the covers, searching for the satin edge of my robe. I was halfway down the hallway before I managed to find the armholes, but then I stood panting and still in front of Burke's closed door, afraid of scaring him further by barging in. Maybe he was just disoriented from partially waking in an unfamiliar room.

Tuppence's nails clicked on the wooden stairs as she trotted to join me. Her rough fur prickling against my bare leg offered the solidity of companionship. Then she sat on my foot and whined.

All was silent again on the other side of the door. "I don't know," I whispered down to her. "What should I do?"

I heard the mattress in our room creak as Pete sat up, then a muted thump as a foot or two hit the floor. "Babe?" he called softly.

I had my mouth open to whisper a reply when the keening started eerily again. Burke wasn't fully awake. He couldn't be. The noise was far too incoherent—a soul-piercing form of terrified.

I quickly turned the knob and eased the door open. "Burke? Burke, honey, it's Meredith. I'm coming in." I had no idea if he was afraid of monsters under the bed or any of the other pernicious childhood myths that seem so deeply embedded in their fertile imaginations.

He was a curled lump under the covers, only his face visible in the small crack of moonlight that crept around the edge of the window shade. His eyes were open but unseeing, and his mouth was stretched in an agonized grimace. The unearthly keening continued and was just about my undoing. It seemed he was completely unaware of my presence.

I scooted onto the bed beside him and gathered him up in my arms, quilts and all. I tucked his head under my chin and started rocking, holding him for all I was worth.

The hall light clicked on, and Pete's silhouette appeared in the doorway. "Babe?"

"I don't know what to do," I whimpered, still rocking.

Pete came in and placed a heavy hand on Burke's head, studying the boy's face in the dim light. "He'll come around. Let's try food." And with that, he bent and lifted Burke from my lap, cradling him up against his chest.

I preceded Pete and his precious cargo down to the kitchen, turning on more lights as I went. Then I swished around, starting the coffeemaker and rummaging in the fridge for anything that might tempt a hungry boy.

But it was Tuppence who successfully nudged Burke out of his waking nightmare. As soon as Pete had sat down, she'd placed her front paws on the edge of his chair and stretched to stick her nose right into the middle of the bundled quilts that encased Burke in his arms. And sneezed. And snorted. Then sneezed some more. Messy, splatty sneezes that make you feel as though you need to take a shower after you've been blessed with one.

The technique that was so effective at rousting gophers out of their burrows had the same effect on Burke. He struggled to free his arms from the cocoon, blinking and bleary-eyed, his shaggy hair a tousled mess.

Pete adjusted him on his lap but kept the boy secure in a strong embrace. "You hungry?" he asked, his voice thick and scratchy.

Burke nodded sleepily and slumped back against Pete's chest as though exhausted.

Just like that he seemed recovered. I had so many questions burning on my tongue. So many things I needed to know. But Pete was right to address Burke's physical needs first.

Hot cocoa and a roast beef sandwich for Burke. Coffee and a roast beef sandwich for Pete. Coffee for me. In that order. Slabs of pie to follow shortly for the man and the boy. I had no appetite.

For the first time since I'd known Burke, he ate slowly—tentatively even—casting worried glances at me out from under his long eyelashes.

"Can you tell us what you were dreaming about, Burke?" Pete finally asked in a soothing rumble.

Burke swiped a blob of mayonnaise with the sourdough crust of his sandwich and stuck it in his mouth. "Missing my dad," he whispered around the wad of bread.

Understandable, definitely. But was that all?

Pete was on my wavelength, because he tried again. "Are you worried about anything?"

I bit my lip and nodded at Pete over Burke's head. He hadn't suggested the words *afraid* or *scared* even though Burke's subconscious behavior had indicated absolute terror far beyond the expected grief. It seemed like it would be better to let the boy acknowledge his own feelings, if we could get him to. But I was no therapist, so I toyed with the handle of my mug and tried to wait patiently.

Burke swallowed the big lump of dough, his eyes watering with the effort. "Where will I live?" he asked in a small voice.

"With Meredith and me," Pete replied promptly. "If you want to. That part hasn't changed. We have lots of room here."

I was tearing up again. What was it with me and waterworks lately? Surely it wasn't hormones? Maybe it was the sight of my husband being so gentle. That wasn't a surprise—he was gentle with me too, but to see him with a child in his arms...I scrubbed my face with the lapel of my robe, pretending my eyes were itchy.

"Burke, you can talk to us," Pete carried on, holding that low, mesmerizing tone that usually makes me want to spill my guts. I hoped it worked on Burke too. "You were up on Gifford Mountain by yourself for a long time. That had to be difficult. You're a brave kid."

Pete couldn't see Burke's face, but I could. And he'd hit something with his prodding. Those mineral blue-green eyes darted and hollowed out, as though retracting into themselves with fear, the pupils huge. Burke's body followed suit, curling deeper into Pete's chest.

There was no safer place to be. Pete's arms tightened around the boy as we shared another knowing glance.

I got up and went around to kneel beside Pete's chair so I could be at eye level with Burke. "We hope you can be happy here," I said, rubbing the knobby little knee closest to me. "And you can tell us anything. You're not in trouble. You didn't do anything wrong. Sheriff Marge, Harriet, Frankie, Jim Carter"—I tried to remember all the people he'd met so far in Platts Landing—"are all here to help you. We really like having kids around," I added with a smile.

And got nothing.

I didn't want to distress him further by continuing to stare at him, so I rose with creaking knees and started clearing away the dirty dishes. Tuppence was still glued to the edge of Pete's chair, whiskers quivering and ears alert, remarkably untempted by the promise of new crumbs on the kitchen floor.

And Pete just held our frightened boy. Solid, strong, steady. Have I mentioned lately how much I love my husband? He always seems to know exactly what to do. His sheer presence should count tenfold for the amount of quiet confidence it conveys.

I had my hands in sudsy water by the time anyone spoke again. There'd seemed no point in rushing back to bed since I was certain Pete and I would just lie there staring at the ceiling, wondering what else we could do for Burke, and Burke risked a return to his nightmare.

Besides, I find washing dishes to be a therapeutic and pacifying task.

"Do bad people always go to jail?" Burke's faint whisper held a tang of pleading.

My hands froze in the warm water, but I was loathe to turn around and face those earnest eyes. Because the truth wasn't the answer I wanted to give him.

But Pete said it anyway. "No. Not always."

I was boring a hole into Pete's reflection on the window above the sink, willing him to add some reassurance to that purely factual statement. Clearly, Burke had something heavy on his mind.

"The police do their best," Pete added on cue, in his deep rumble, "but they don't always know everything. Their job is to find all the pieces that prove someone is guilty, and sometimes that's not possible."

"There are a lot of bad people out there," Burke said, his words muffled by the quilt that had crept up around his chin.

"Yep," Pete agreed.

What could I add to that? Nothing. I was overwhelmed with sadness that our boy already had such a close acquaintance with the evils of this world.

~oOo~

Pete informed me that he was going out with Sheriff Marge and her crew to help with the search for the Brightbill cabin on Gifford Mountain while we were still stretched under the quilts in our bed.

"But you had a job scheduled for today?" I said in the pre-dawn gloom, not really meaning it. Of course Pete could take care of himself, so why was I suffering a twinge of worry and nerves over the idea that he'd be traipsing through the forest in a remote corner of the county—along with a whole contingent of armed officers of the law—on a frigid winter day?

"We need answers," he rumbled in my ear, pulling me closer in our warm nest. "Whatever it takes to set Burke's mind at ease. The kid's terrified."

I pressed my face into Pete's shoulder, inhaling the yummy licorice and dusty wheat scent that lingers on his skin even after he's showered. "I know," I whispered.

"Besides, that derelict barge has been anchored outside the main channel for ages. As long as it's not sinking, Paulson Lumber won't care when I tow it to the scrap yard. Until the Coast Guard gets on their case, that is."

One of the perks of being self-employed—a flexible schedule. So he was free to swap things around so he could offer assistance in resolving a far more important matter. I slid my hand around the back of his neck and pulled him in for a warm, deep, drowsy kiss. "Be careful," I whispered. "Things happen on Gifford Mountain."

CHAPTER 9

Same old, same old—sort of. Providing a routine for Burke seemed like a good idea. I didn't tell him where Pete had gone, and he didn't ask as he stumbled sleepily into the kitchen and hauled his bony little self up onto a chair for the big, hot breakfast I was dishing up.

From the way she staggered wearily, her front and back halves working their syncopated and only loosely affiliated way down the stairs at Burke's heels, I assumed Tuppence had spent the remainder of the night with him after Pete had carried him upstairs once he'd fallen asleep again. Not just in Burke's room, but up on the bed and stretched out beside him, like a canine nanny. Officially against the house rules for pets, but I wasn't quibbling, as long as Burke didn't mind her snoring.

If it was possible, my hound was more worried about the boy than I was. She parked herself under the table by his dangling feet instead of imbibing in her usual habit of licking fresh bacon grease splatters off the floor in front of the stove.

So it was a good thing preparations for the wedding reception were ramping up at the museum. I'd been anticipating a hectic day even before I'd had the additional worry about the search on Gifford Mountain ratcheted into the back of my mind.

Pete had warned me that most of Gifford Mountain had spotty cell phone reception at best, but he'd promised to call or text when he could—when or if anything was discovered.

Lingering seemed pointless. Small talk wasn't an option. So Burke and I moved like automatons through our morning preparations and ended up at the museum's locked front doors two hours before opening time. Even so, Frankie had beat us there.

I found her in the mansion's kitchen, which doubled as a staff breakroom, chewing the eraser end of a pencil and frowning mightily at her clipboard, a mug of steaming coffee at her elbow. She looked as though she'd slept about as much as I had, and pitched her brows at me without comment as I pointed Burke in the direction of the hot cocoa packets. Soothing the kid with sugar, or something like that, but he was a long way from being pudgy. And he'd returned to the weighty silence of his early time with us.

I tipped my head toward the door. "Want to look at the seating chart one last time?" I asked.

Frankie took the hint and shoved her chair back from the table.

She followed me to the gift shop and spoke first. "Henry's on the search team. He told me Pete's going too?" She fiddled with the jeweled zipper tab on her knit jacket. Her hands always revealed the energetic state of her mind. She might be amazingly efficient, but the woman could not sit—or stand—still.

I nodded, surprised and pleased to hear that her suitor was lending his expertise—if not his helicopter—to the search. Gifford Mountain was too heavily wooded for aerial viewing to be of much benefit.

"Who else, do you know?" I asked. I hadn't wanted to bother Sheriff Marge with silly questions about her methods just to appease my worried imagination.

Frankie was a font of information. She ticked names off on her fingers. "Herb Tinsley, Julian Joseph, Amos Stanley."

I let out a breath I didn't know I'd been holding and nodded. Adding Pete and Henry to the list, it was an excellent roster—knowledgeable, experienced men; some were older, but all quite spry for their ages and incredibly dedicated. Sheriff Marge was tapping into their collective wisdom, and I was grateful for their willingness to help.

Frankie stretched out a hand and squeezed my forearm. "The main concern is the weather," she said, seeming to echo my thoughts. "A storm front's moving in. They're predicting two to three inches of snowfall by midnight—more at higher elevations, plus another few inches tomorrow. It'll dip down into the teens overnight up on Gifford Mountain," she added, her brown eyes wide.

"They won't get stuck up there," I said, louder than I'd meant to—probably trying to reassure both of us. "Or lost. They have GPS, radios, and decades—no, centuries—of common sense among them."

Frankie cracked a little chuckle. "Well, when you put it that way..."

"So, you're going to keep us busy today, right?" I blurted, getting down to business. I explained briefly about Burke's nightmare, and added, "I hope he'll sleep better tonight if he's absolutely exhausted. Me too, so put us to work."

"That," Frankie replied, tapping her clipboard with a rueful shake of her helmet hair, "will not be a problem."

~oOo~

They hit pay dirt with the seventh cabin they investigated. *Stumbled upon* would probably have been a

67

better term, but admitting that degree of pure chance in an official police report wasn't exactly standard protocol. Deputy Owen Hobart figured his boss just might do it anyway. If anyone stuck to the unvarnished version of the truth, it was Sheriff Marge.

The first three cabins they'd rifled through had been obviously abandoned years ago. The fourth had a family of disgruntled owls in residence. The fifth showed signs of recent—and hastily vacated—use, but no indicators that one of the occupants had been (or still was) a minor. Sheriff Marge had a philosophy of live and let live in that situation—although she'd carefully noted the cabin's GPS coordinates in her notebook for possible future reference—so they'd resumed their roving search, making sure to create a great deal of noise as they left the vicinity. The sixth cabin also fit into the long-abandoned and holes-in-the-roof-so-big-you-could-see-the-stars category.

Who knew so many hidey-holes of a human nature were tucked into camouflaged hollows and against jagged knolls in the deep woods? Owen was certainly surprised, although he wasn't going to be flapping his gums about it anytime soon.

Hard to, at any rate, because his teeth were ground together to keep them from chattering. There was something else he'd never tell anyone—that he was wearing two layers of *silk* long underwear under all his other gear. Better than the highly engineered synthetic stuff that was all the rage among his buddies. Moisture-wicking properties, his ass. But even the silk wasn't quite doing the job of cushioning his ballistic vest today, and he could feel a blister rising at the edge of the vest under his right armpit.

But compared to the extra weight of the ceramic plates he may or may not have inserted into his vest when he went on nightly raids in Afghanistan, his current situation was tolerable. The plates worked—mostly—but they'd added a cumbersome bulk that slowed you down, especially if you were trying to be stealthy, which was *all* the time out in that godforsaken wasteland. A place he never wanted to return to—a place many of his friends had returned from in body bags.

Today's search was more his style—the dripping, towering trees and the thick canopy of needled branches over his head; the silent duff of rampant moss and ivy tendrils under his boots; the slick, rocky crags of volcanic basalt that seemed to rise out of nowhere, left behind by a massive cataclysmic event; and the twittering little birds that were mostly invisible in the dense foliage. A man could get accustomed to this.

He'd been scrambling up and down over steep, tumbled boulder fields and following icy freshets since sunup along with the other searchers. Sitting in a patrol car most of his days was certainly taking its toll on his otherwise ripped physique. Hitting the weights hard couldn't compensate for a steady diet of sedentary vigilance. So he was panting—subtly—and reveling in the strenuous movement, sucking in that good burn in his quadriceps, hamstrings, and calves even if it was temporarily uncomfortable.

Sheriff Marge emerged from the cabin and stood on the stoop—if one could call the artfully concentric pad of round river rock that fanned out like a mosaic on the ground in front of the doorway as a stoop—blinking against the slash of cold, gray daylight that shafted in through the tree branches, and tipped her chin at him.

He'd known it before she'd rapped on the door and then stuck her head in and then disappeared fully inside and stayed there for twenty minutes. Because none of the other cabins had been decorated in the slightest, none exhibiting anything beyond pure functionality and, in most cases, even the functionality had been subject to interpretation.

But this was the right cabin, the recent abode of one Burke Brightbill and his now deceased father. Sheriff Marge had obviously seen what she needed to inside. So the little squirt had been telling the truth. Pretty good, really. Thinking back to when he'd been eleven years old, he'd had a lot of survival reasons for stretching the truth. The Army had been his saving grace, coming in just the nick of time. So it was refreshing to learn of a kid who had no such need or compunction to lie, no such rough background—figuratively. Because literally, it was still rough, the decorative stoop notwithstanding.

Owen returned Sheriff Marge's nod and signaled to his assigned team—Henry Parker and Pete Sills. They'd check a widening perimeter, see what they could find, if anything, while Sheriff Marge and her crew combed through the cabin for clues and packed up any remaining personal belongings.

Little crystal ice granules were falling from the sky, a precursor to the snow in the forecast. They were melting upon impact and then refreezing, coating the rim of his knit cap and the flaps of the pockets on his chest. Wouldn't be long before their footing became even more treacherous. Good thing the guys working with him were experienced.

Owen knelt on one knee and spread the Forest Service map on his broad, meaty thigh as though the surface was a portable writing desk. Henry and Pete huddled over him, and they quickly parsed the search area into segments.

"We'll overlap if we have time," Owen reminded them. But dusk fell quickly in January, and even quicker in the dense forest. "Watch your step." He didn't need to tell them, but he felt better doing it anyway.

Twenty minutes later, he found the first thing he wasn't expecting. A rutted track that wasn't on the Forest Service map. Too narrow for log trucks, and this part of the national forest wasn't under concession anyway. Any logs dragged out of here were essentially poached.

But somebody had been driving a pickup along the muddy track, and not that long ago. The tread marks were still fairly clear in a few sections where the track was protected by dense overhanging branches. Nothing unusual about the marks—standard sized truck tires, not those gargantuan, extra-knobby ones favored by off-road enthusiasts. Even though that was the typical person Owen imagined would be prowling through the woods with enough observant attention to find this track in the first place—they were a pretty die-hard bunch, those off-roaders. The driver had been somebody who knew the area well—or who was almost irreparably lost.

That second scenario worried him the most.

He had his phone out and was snapping reference photos of the tread-imprinted mud when Pete Sills shouted his name.

CHAPTER 10

It was a woman. She'd shaved her legs.

Not that Owen was an expert in female personal hygiene, but it seemed to him that if a woman lived in a cabin like the ones they'd spent the day sweeping through, she probably wouldn't have taken the care or had the proper amenities to indulge in that degree of grooming.

Owen had no idea why he noted that particular fact first. Maybe because she'd had nice legs—runner's legs with muscular calves and slender ankles. Still did, even though they were now rather worse for wear, having been gnawed on.

Black bears, probably. But he wouldn't put it past a hungry cougar, either. Predators turned into scavengers quite easily when it was convenient. And that included humans.

Because the woman hadn't been killed by an animal, even though her body had been mauled after the fact. The sharp—and straight—slice across her throat was far too clean to have been made by teeth or claws. That much was clear even though the horrific gash that nearly separated her head from the rest of her body was showing signs of decay.

It'd been cold. Very cold. Still was. Which was a preserving factor where decomposition was concerned. But off the top of his head, some part of Owen's brain—the part that wasn't considering retching—placed her death at a week, maybe up to ten days, ago. His analytical side was already setting a parameter around the scope of the investigation he knew would consume his foreseeable future.

The medical examiner would provide the specifics of how and when, but those details always took a while, and he was going to need to get a jump on this.

This. The scene before him. The one he was still struggling to wrap his whole head around.

His stomach was having a renewed wave of difficulty with it too. Big guys barf. It's maybe not a stereotypical fact, but true nonetheless.

Owen returned from the far side of a convenient bush a minute later, wiping his mouth with the back of his gloved hand, and resumed his place next to Pete Sills.

Pete's expression was unreadable, but the characteristic warmth and humor in his blue gaze were long gone. "Gonna move her yet?" he asked.

Owen shook his head. "Can't," he croaked, then cleared his throat. "Gotta follow procedure, because she sure as heck didn't do that to herself."

"I don't like seeing her there, in the water." Pete's words were clipped, tight, and he shoved his hands into his coat pockets as though to restrain himself from indulging in an irrational, yet charitable, act.

Owen didn't like seeing the woman in her current condition either, regardless of her setting, but he knew what Pete meant. She was exposed, cold. He, too, was fighting the rushing urge to wrap her in a blanket. Not that she was immodest, really, but he just felt that if she were alive, she'd be embarrassed by her position, by her vulnerability, by her raw need for physical comfort that would now never be met.

~oOo~

It was a long slog back to the logging road where they'd parked their vehicles, where they would set up a staging area and command post for processing the crime scene. Pete was checking the signal status on his cell phone every few minutes and punching a speed-dial button whenever he thought he might have half a bar.

In that moment, as they trudged silently together up a steep incline, puffing steam clouds into the bitterly cold air, Owen was glad he didn't have anybody at home who was worrying about the long night ahead of them. About the snow that was quickly filling in their footprints in the gathering dusk. About the gruesome investigation. Nope. Some things were easier solo, and being a deputy sheriff was one of them.

In other circumstances, and perhaps in a different frame of mind, he would've envied Pete, who'd managed to put a ring on the only single woman in Sockeye County who was worth settling down for. He was trying to call Meredith so he could forewarn her, since the orphaned boy was currently in her care.

That thought alone swerved Owen's brown study back into its somber professional trajectory. Because the boy, if he'd been telling the truth about "holding down the fort" for his father seven to ten days ago—and there was no reason to doubt him at this point—most likely could not have avoided also seeing the macabre corpse stranded on the pebbled bank of the stream that tumbled down a little ravine not more than a tenth of a mile from his cabin.

The big question was, what else had Burke seen?

~oOo~

It felt as though a giant fist had cratered my lung cavity. I spun around with the phone pressed to my ear, checking behind me even though I knew Burke was upstairs with Frankie. Then I tipped a shoulder into one of the support posts that had been doing a great job, for over a century, of keeping the Imogene's main floor from collapsing into the basement. I hoped it could hold me up as well.

"How sure are you?" I whispered.

"Babe..." Pete's weary tone was edged with finality.

"I'm sorry," I murmured. "Dumb question. What am I supposed to do—or say?"

"Nothing yet. Sheriff Marge has to question Burke again, obviously. Figure out what he saw or didn't see. For now, though, she wants you to not let on about anything being amiss up at the cabin. Just carry on like normal."

I made a strangled sound and hugged the support post tighter.

"I know, Babe," Pete said. "I know." He was breathing heavily into the phone.

So I turned my attention to his condition. "How are you?"

"Fine," he replied curtly. Of course he wasn't going to complain about the logistically—not to mention emotionally and physically—challenging task ahead of the entire search-turned-recovery team. Or about what he'd found on the stream bank.

I also knew this call was one of the rare few that would be possible to receive from the team during the long coming night, so I had to make the most of it for my dear friends' sakes as well. "Is Henry okay? And Herb? I can tell Frankie and Harriet, right? They'll be worrying otherwise."

"Yeah, babe, you can take care of everybody on your end, but Sheriff Marge wants it kept quiet." There was a rough cough, and then he added, "Just stay safe for me, will you? I love you..."

As I recognized the hashy clicking sound of the call being dropped, I couldn't help feeling that I'd failed Burke before I'd even met him. I knew Pete hadn't told me everything about what he'd encountered up there on Gifford Mountain—and he might not ever fill in those gaps for me, protective husband that he was. But with what little I did know, I couldn't fathom how a child could deal with that sort of scenario.

~oOo~

I don't know how I held it together. The one thing I had going for me was that Burke didn't know me well. So the odd hitches in my voice and my scattered, spastic attention lapses perhaps weren't as obvious to him as they were to me. It was surreal, trying to observe my own behavior from inside my head and wrangle it into some semblance of normalcy—whatever that is. I hadn't really had to strain to meet such an objective before, and the concentration it required exhausted me.

Tuppence spent the night sprawled on Burke's bed again, and as far as I could tell, he didn't have a repeat of the waking nightmare. I don't think I actually slept, however, listening for any squeak or murmur that might leak under his bedroom door. Mostly what I heard into the wee hours—in the regular cadence of a contented slumber—were Tuppence's snores. But if Burke could tolerate her obnoxious nocturnal emissions—and at such close range—then so could I, from the distance of the hallway.

The one thing that remained unfailingly constant was Burke's appetite. He chowed through oatmeal with maple syrup and pecans, scrambled eggs, sausages, hash browns with diced onions and red peppers, grape juice, and hot cocoa. When he asked, around a mouthful, where Pete was—my husband's second morning's absence from the breakfast table apparently being noteworthy to his young mind—I replied that Pete was working.

Which I had no doubt about. Working unflinchingly through the long, cold night, preserving a crime scene and likely serving as a pack mule for all the equipment that had to be shuttled in and then shuttled back out again.

As a matter of course, Pete *was* gone a lot, for his regular job. From Burke's novice perspective, there was no reason this particular morning should feel any different from those to come—if he chose to stay with us—no matter how knotted into hard lumps my stomach was. At least, that's what I kept telling myself as I barely sipped my coffee and washed dishes, even though I knew Burke had been abandoned once before by a respected male figure in his life. No reason for him to see things differently now. I was grateful the boy's ravenous state made packaging up any leftover breakfast food unnecessary.

Rupert had rejoined the land of the only-slightly-sniffly living and greeted us in the Imogene's parking lot as we all disembarked from our vehicles. We scuffed through the thin layer of snow that had dusted the pavement overnight, and he caught my eye above Burke's head, giving me a short, agreeable nod. I'd texted him the bare-bones facts of Burke's constantly evolving situation the previous evening.

"How's the new exhibit coming along?" Rupert asked.

I nodded my appreciation to him. Nothing like a good curatorial task to redirect my frazzled thoughts. "It's requiring extensive sifting," I replied. "As far as I can tell, Sheriff Marge dumped about a hundred and twenty years' worth of county law enforcement history on us. Not everything is worth fleshing out for a full display."

Fleshing maybe wasn't the best word, considering the picture I had in my mind of the scene on Gifford Mountain, and I winced slightly. Pete had been exceedingly careful with his brief description on the phone, but my imagination is noted for its unbridled exuberance.

Good man that he is, Rupert pretended not to notice my queasiness. "So, Burke," he said jovially, tapping the boy on the shoulder, "fancy a rummage through the Gilded Age?"

I cocked a brow at my boss, and he grinned back at me.

"I seem to recall a few Pinkerton items in my possession," he clarified. "Could enhance the exhibit," he added with a nonchalant shrug. But there was a glint in his eye—he was very aware that he was baiting me, dangling such a tantalizing prospect just out of reach.

I nearly laughed aloud, and a tingling sensation flittered through the muscles of my rib cage—producing a surprising lightness that I no longer took for granted after the heavy news of the past several days. Because Rupert's office—which contains his personal collection that's separate from the Imogene's official holdings—is a disaster zone of epic proportions. If I'd thought searching through the basement for the remembered coroner's kit was a good day's work, then trying to find a particular item of personal memorabilia in Rupert's office was about a hundred times more rigorous. And just the thing for a curious boy.

"Pinkerton, huh?" I yawned, feigning bored disinterest, delighted that the small boy beside me was also responding—if quietly—with bright-eyed acuity. Maybe we share a curiosity gene.

Rupert nodded his large bald head and the tweed driving cap perched on top above ears that were reddened with cold. "The one and the same." As though muttering to himself as he unlocked the museum's front doors, he added, "The renowned private detective agency that served as a precursor for the FBI. Their agents were brave and sneaky, employing cutting-edge technology for their day. Controversial, too, and the reason some of our laws exist—as a response to abuses of power in the absence of specific regulations at the time."

And an important epoch in American history. Leave it to Rupert to combine the promise of an alluring treasure hunt with a dose of facts and illustrative consequences. Then again, that professorial combination characterized the entirety of Rupert's life—he was an inveterate bargain-hunter, flea-market-aficionado, minutiae-preserving relic-scrounger, and cultural-ramification-expounder in his own right.

I was still grinning as I saw the boys off to their adventures on the third floor at the doors of the freight elevator, then wandered into the gift shop where a chapped-cheek Frankie was just unwrapping herself from several woolen layers.

"Oh honey," were her first words, and she bundled me into a sudden breath-squashing hug. "I'm so sorry."

"For what?" I gasped, my lungs still compressed.

"Well, I don't know," she admitted, pulling away and readjusting the embroidered hem of her fitted jacket with fidgeting fingers. "For Burke, I guess. For you not being able to talk to him about...well, about *it*—yet. For Henry and Pete and the whole search team still up on Gifford Mountain in this storm..." She squinted and turned her worried gaze out the window where the snow had resumed falling, soft and gently ominous.

"It's okay," I said quietly, trying to hide my pleased smile. "I'll gladly serve as a proxy hug-ee until you have Henry back in your arms."

"Oh!" She reddened, and pressed a hand to her bosom. "That's not what I was doing—was it? I do miss him. But we're not...I mean, we're *old*—" She pronounced the term with nose-wrinkled chagrin, as though having a long and experienced life was a disease. "And we're taking it slow and"—she shook her helmet hair, trying, no doubt, to reassert calculated logic's dominance over blatant, and obvious to everyone but her, infatuation—"well, we're just friends, enjoying each other's company from time to time."

"Uh-huh," I grunted, now completely unable to suppress a mischievous smirk. The lady doth protest too much. "Tell that to Henry. Want to bet who has the next wedding in Sockeye County?" I suggested, with a knowing wink. "The next one, after tomorrow, that is?"

But Frankie just groaned and snatched her omnipresent clipboard off the counter. "Don't remind me."

CHAPTER 11

As it had been many times before, the kitchen at the Imogene Museum ended up being the location of a weighty and gut-wrenching conference. The old mansion had seen her share of woe.

But at least we had bitterly strong coffee and an abundant supply of hot cocoa packets for the participants.

Sheriff Marge was the first to arrive, toward the middle of the afternoon. She hooked my elbow in her strong grip and pulled me away from my task of arranging centerpieces on all the round tables set up along the periphery of the ballroom—enough to accommodate almost three hundred hungry guests.

"You'll have to be in there with me," she said gruffly, "since Burke doesn't have a parent present. An unbiased advocate who can flag me down if I ask something inappropriate."

I quickly glanced at her frowning face, startled. "How would you ask anything inappropriate?" My voice squeaked a bit. Sheriff Marge is nothing if not conscientious in her job.

And that was the very reason for her concern. "He's not just a minor, he's *very* young. And I have every reason to expect he's seen something horrifying. I'm shaken up about it myself." She pulled off her Stratton hat to swipe her sleeve across her brow. "I have to make sure any evidence I collect—and that includes potential witness testimony—is admissible in court. Questioning a child without an unbiased, adult advocate present isn't prudent."

"I'm hardly unbiased," I murmured, my fists clenched at my sides.

"You're all he has right now, Meredith. Step up to the plate," she growled. "It's more than just room and board you're offering the kid. It's shelter, especially emotional shelter. There'll be more nightmares, I know." Her voice softened, but those steel-gray eyes never left my face. "I hate it too. But *this*"—she flapped a thick hand to indicate the situation up on Gifford Mountain—"has to be resolved. I can't let murderers run amok in my county, not even to spare the boy."

I flushed with embarrassment. I knew that—of course I did. It was just a massive, monstrous, terrifying responsibility—this caring for a child in all the needful ways. And I had no training, no competency. I was going to screw up royally; I already knew that. It was just a matter of when, and how many countless times. But under the weight of her stern glare, I nodded somberly.

She squeezed my arm in response. She also wasn't a grandmother for nothing. There truly was no better person to be asking these hard questions than Sheriff Marge. I'd rather be on her team than anywhere else.

I trudged upstairs to retrieve Burke from Rupert's office. Both of them—even Rupert in his Humpty-Dumpty-esque, less-than-elastic state—were kneeling on the floor with an array of knickknacks and newspaper clippings spread around them. As far as I could tell, no order had been wrought among Rupert's multitudinous jumbled treasures, but Burke's eyes were shining in spite of the shaggy hair he was perpetually brushing out of his line of sight. I hated very much that I had to interrupt the educational scavenger hunt.

"Will you need more assistance later?" I asked Rupert.

He understood my meaning instantly. "Absolutely. I'm afraid we got distracted and have yet to locate the box that might contain the Pinkerton items." Rupert creaked slowly to standing—which caused his face to turn an alarming shade of fuchsia—and cast a blank glance around his office.

The former guest suite of sitting room, bedroom, and (non-functioning for flood-prevention reasons, the pipes not having been retrofitted since the old girl was built in 1902) bathroom would've been spacious and even elegant if it hadn't been piled—in many places nearly to the crown molding against the high ceiling—with an utter disarray of mismatched storage containers, papers, boxes, scabby pieces of furniture that doubled as shelves, rolled-up rugs and cardboard tubes containing either artwork or blueprints or...I could hardly guess. There were narrow pathways a person could barely edge through to get from one room to another, a hoarder's paradise.

"It'll come to you," I murmured.

Rupert chuckled ruefully. "I'm afraid you know me too well, my dear." But then a flicker of inspiration crossed his sweaty face. "Ah-ha!" He pointed a stubby finger toward the leaning tower of Pisa behind his desk. "Perhaps in those celluloid cartons."

I didn't understand the logic behind that assumption, but I also knew better than to ask. Instead, I offered a wobbly smile to Burke, and tipped my head toward the door.

We left Rupert happily humming to himself while trying to finagle one box out of the stack, much like the game of Jenga, only bigger and with historical artifacts as building blocks. It was a challenge of gravitational physics that I was grateful I didn't have to watch, only hoping that we wouldn't have to rescue Rupert from a resulting avalanche.

Sheriff Marge always looks tired. But today her awkwardly slumped form—still stiff in the middle due to her ballistic vest—and elbows plonked heavily on the table in front of her presented a new low in that characteristic. I assumed she hadn't slept overnight. The Styrofoam cup of coffee in front of her wasn't going to cut it, but I didn't have anything more substantial to offer her. I'd sent our brown-bagged snacks upstairs with Burke that morning, and I assumed they'd been devoured in short order.

Unless...I pulled my phone from my pocket and fired off a quick text to Frankie.

After directing Burke toward a metal folding chair opposite from Sheriff Marge, I stepped up to the long counter and began the requisite preparation of a packet of hot cocoa. I made one for myself too, needing the sugar boost and dopamine hit.

I kept glancing over my shoulder at the pair of them, thinking the sooner we could get this over with, the better. But Sheriff Marge was silent and seemingly engrossed in studying the tendrils of steam that wafted off her coffee while Burke was hunched in his chair, hands wedged under his thighs while his feet swung freely, only the tip of one shoelace actually dragging on the black and white tiled floor, and his profile wholly obscured by his mop of hair.

He was so small. So very small.

I hurried, and noisily slid out a seat for myself after depositing the cocoas on the table.

Sheriff Marge cleared her throat and clicked a button on a small black gadget that she'd propped in the middle of the table—an altogether different type of centerpiece.

She rattled off all our names as the people present and the date and time.

Then she heaved a great sigh. "Burke," she said steadily, gently, "we found your cabin today, and packed up most of your things. You had a lot of books up there."

To that, Burke nodded, and he peeked up at her from under the fringe of hair.

"You dad was a professor?" she queried.

Burke nodded again.

"Son, please answer audibly." Sheriff Marge pointed at the eavesdropping gadget. "This thing is pretty good, but it can't hear silent."

"Yeah," Burke whispered.

"How long had you been living up on Gifford Mountain?"

"Since I was eight," he whispered.

I nudged the cup of cocoa closer to him, worried that he hadn't even acknowledged its existence yet when edibles usually had such an extremely short shelf life in his vicinity.

"About two years and three months, then?" Sheriff Marge prodded.

My eyes widened. It sounded like she knew Burke's birth date, to be so precise. And about the instigating factor that had prompted Burke's father to flee civilization.

She just shook her weary head at me with a faint trace of an exhausted smile. *Not now*, she was sending out on our merged wavelength, *don't ask me now*.

My body language must've been easy to read. I bit my lip and leaned back in the seat, pretending I was comfortable when all my muscles were screaming to fidget. What else did she know?

"So you were holding the fort for your dad?" Sheriff Marge continued, not really waiting for Burke's reply to the previous question—not necessary, I supposed, when she already knew the answer.

Burke nodded again, silent. But then he ventured, "You saw her, didn't you?" And he was gazing steadfastly at the worn and weary woman across from him.

It was Sheriff Marge's turn to nod. "She was still there. We're taking care of her now."

"I tried to," Burke whispered. "But she was—" His little body spasmed and a haunted expression gripped his features, turning those big mineral eyes into fathomless, ageless depths of sorrow.

I scooted over and wrapped an arm around him.

"She was dead," he finished simply, leaning against me.

Then he was burrowing into me, clinging desperately, giant hiccuping sobs racking his little body.

I had an armful—a lapful—of devastated boy, a lead anchor of grief that was sinking into my own soul. I had no barriers against this kind of pain, and I realized I was shedding my own tears into his hair.

"Did you know her?" Sheriff Marge persisted a minute later, after she'd slugged her coffee, removed her perpetual reading glasses, and dragged her fingers across her eyelids before resettling the glasses. She was resolute. This had to be done—the questioning.

Burke shook his head, his face mashed against my collarbone. I wasn't letting go of him for anything.

"The witness is shaking his head in the negative," Sheriff Marge murmured for the benefit of the recorder. "When did you first see her?"

"When she got out of the pickup truck. With those two men."

Sheriff Marge shifted. It was subtle, but Burke's answer disturbed her. Was it not what she'd been expecting? And his words reminded me of that non-sequitur question he'd asked earlier—if bad people always went to jail. Had he been testing to see if he could trust Pete and me with the dreadful knowledge he carried?

"Did she seem afraid, worried?" Sheriff Marge asked.

Again Burke rubbed his head against my collarbone as he reclined against me. I was going to get a groove there. "Not at first. But later, yes. She screamed."

"Okay, Burke," Sheriff Marge finally uttered, after the horror of his short comment had sunk in. "I want you to tell me everything you saw and heard that day, from the very beginning. We'll go slow, and you can think about it. I'm hoping that if we do it this one time, you won't have to worry about it ever again. But I need your help to catch those men. Can you do that for me, and for the lady who was killed?"

She was holding his gaze solemnly across the table, and it was like two ageless depths had met their match. I was the lone spectator and witness to their grave agreement when Burke finally rubbed his head the other way on my collarbone—up and down.

CHAPTER 12

Pete came in a few minutes later, the wrapped sandwiches I'd asked Frankie to order in his hands.

Dennis Durante, the owner and pseudo-chef of Willow Oaks, a vineyard and wine-tasting facility on the banks of the Columbia River that also happened to house a wood-fired oven and small restaurant, was doing the catering for the wedding reception. He'd been in and out of the museum all day, getting things set up, so I'd hoped he'd also be able to provide us with a little extra sustenance on short notice. He'd come through with flying colors.

Surprisingly—or maybe not—Burke was able to devour a sandwich while also providing the gruesome play-by-play of that day on Gifford Mountain. That day the woman had been killed. As though his stomach was made of iron.

Mine wasn't, and I only picked at my pastrami with provolone, sprouts and creamy dill aioli on sourdough while still cradling the ravenous boy in my arms. Pete had settled beside me, with his free arm resting along the back of my chair.

Pete smelled tired—a strange combination of pine sap and fresh air and sweat and car exhaust and a plastic-y odor, like the fumes put off by a new tent—or maybe that's the peculiar scent of body bags. I shuddered, and his hand clamped warmly on my shoulder. We certainly made a bizarre picture of a family unit, the three of us.

But the boy on my lap was already demonstrating inexplicable resilience, keeping up his end of the hard bargain he and Sheriff Marge had agreed upon.

"Black," he replied, his mouth full. "The pickup was black, a Dodge Ram, with a tiny gold pinstripe running down the whole length and no tailgate."

Have I mentioned that Burke misses nothing? That fact was apparently just as true eleven days prior as it was in that moment, as he recited pristine details with ease. He'd provided the date and a very close estimate of the time when the pickup and its occupants had intruded into the peaceful valley where he'd been patiently waiting for his father to return.

Sheriff Marge was scritching madly in her notebook, also ignoring her sandwich, as though the recorder wasn't fully reliable and that somehow seeing Burke's testimony in blue ink would make the clues line up in logical order in her mind.

"Old? Dented?" Sheriff Marge prompted, and in so doing described about ninety percent of the vehicles in Sockeye County.

But Burke shook his head. "Pretty new. Dirty on the lower parts because it'd been driven on logging roads, but shiny above the splatters, like it'd been waxed or something."

"Washington plates?"

Burke had to think for a moment—I felt his little rib cage expand against mine with a deep breath—then he said, his voice smaller. "Yes, but I don't know the number."

Sheriff Marge squinted at him briefly, as though testing his veracity, then returned to her vigorous note taking. "No problem. Tell me about the people inside the pickup."

"Two men and the...and the...lady," he finally said.

"What were they talking about?" Sheriff Marge was artful in her verification, sliding in second and third questions that didn't seem tedious but served to confirm or clarify his earlier statements.

"Hiking. How beautiful it is in the forest. The lady was learning to navigate with a compass."

"And then what happened?"

"They went around to the back of the pickup to get their gear, and the men—well one of the men grabbed her arms and pinned them against her side, and the other man forced a loop of cord over her head."

Pete had warned me—a little—about the mode of death, but Burke's simple, and necessarily brutal, explanation—because the act was unspeakably brutal— still shocked the breath out of me. It'd been so fast, so unexpected. If I was surprised, no wonder the as yet unnamed lady had been. At least she hadn't suffered unduly, if I could even think such a thing about murder.

But Burke's next words stomped that wishful, euphemistic idea right out of my mind. "Then the men got back in the pickup, and drove really fast."

"They dragged the lady?" From her tone, I could tell Sheriff Marge already knew what came next.

He nodded.

And the cord had been thin—not a rope—so her head, as Pete had told me, was nearly severed with the sudden, slicing force. If Burke hadn't been on my lap, I might've made a dash for the restroom and lost the little bit of sandwich I'd eaten. As it was, I swallowed down the rising bile and concentrated on the tickly locks of Burke's hair that were brushing my neck.

Burke had seen this in real life—in real time, and I was the one falling apart with only what my imagination could supply. I hugged him closer and squeezed my eyes shut against the onslaught of images of a woman being yanked off her feet by the neck.

To my great relief, Sheriff Marge changed direction with her next questions. "What did the men look like? Did you hear either of them refer to each other by name?"

"No names. I don't even know the lady's name." Burke kept coming back to her—and why wouldn't he? He was just a little boy, but a strong protective nature would be key to his development into a man. So how could this event *not* scar him for life? I didn't want to think about the ramifications of that.

"The guy driving had a big belly that made his clothes tight, and he was wearing a camouflage down coat and those slick pants that are waterproof. The other guy was in jeans and dark-blue coat with a zipper up the front," Burke said.

"Shoes?"

"Boots. Both of them."

"Gloves?"

Burke nodded. "It was cold. They were dressed for the weather." An understatement, surely, but his matter-of-factness reminded me of the survival mode he'd been living in for the past couple years.

"Was the lady dressed for the weather?"

"Yes, but they took some of her clothes off—after."

"Explain that part to me," Sheriff Marge requested gently.

Burke's little voice became strained. "She was wearing those waterproof pants too, and they pulled them off. She had those black legging things, skinny ones that are tight, on underneath…the kind that came to just below her knees."

To my furtive relief, Burke clearly wasn't familiar with ladies' unmentionables, but his description sounded a lot like high-tech long underwear. A prerequisite for responsible backwoods hiking in January. The lady had been no dummy.

"They took off her coat too," Burke was whispering, "and a down vest she had on underneath that. But they left her long-sleeve T-shirt on." He rubbed his eyes with the heels of his hands, and his words became even more muffled. "They had to take off her boots too, and her socks just kind of fell off while they were doing that. Stripes. She had striped socks on. I used to like striped socks, but my last pair got too holey, and even Dad couldn't darn them anymore. He told me that if I unraveled the rest of the yarn into bits, the birds would take it to cushion their nests in the spring."

Why couldn't I breathe? Yet again? These snippets of Burke's life, the deprivation but also the seeming care that had gone into his experience, as though his father had been molding him somehow, grooming him for his future life, and loving him intensely all at the same time. That would be my job now—Pete's and mine, if Burke agreed to it—and I was mentally staggering under the magnitude of the responsibility.

Pete's hand shifted, up under my hair, and he kneaded the back of my neck. Clearly, my panicky thoughts were stamped all over my external expression as well.

"Tell me about the men's faces," Sheriff Marge suggested. "What color hair did they have, and could you see their eye colors?"

"The driver—the big guy—he had dark brown hair under his cap and a mustache and beard that went like this—" Burke drew a line along his own upper lip and down around to his chin and back up with his finger, indicating a goatee. "His eyes were brown, and he had white marks on his face, right here—" This time Burke raised both of his forefingers and pressed them horizontally across the top of his cheekbones just beneath his eyes. "Like maybe he wears sunglasses all summer so the rest of his face is permanently browned except for those spots."

Again, I was floored by the minute specificity of Burke's recollection.

Sheriff Marge grunted with apparent satisfaction as well. "And the other guy?"

"I couldn't see his hair because he had his knit hat pulled down farther, and lighter eyes too—I don't know what color. He was maybe a little older than the other guy, and thinner, and shorter, but strong, because the lady tried to get away from him, and he wouldn't let her go. I think he was the boss."

Sheriff Marge's brows shot up above the rims of her reading glasses. "What makes you say that?"

Burke shrugged against my chest. "He was bossy. Told the other guy what to do."

So simple—and so universal. That innate sense of resistance to being bossed around. I wasn't sure we even had another word for it in English, since bossiness—and the abhorrence of it when applied to ourselves—is so well understood.

But Sheriff Marge had premeditation on her mind. "Did they act like they knew what they were going to do? Or did they stumble around a bit, figuring things out? Did either of them swear or get mad at the other?"

"They knew exactly what they were doing," Burke whispered. "Like they had a plan. Only the lady was surprised. They didn't talk about what they were going to do next; they just did it."

It all seemed so remote. And yet so real. How do you guard against something like this? How do you raise a shield around the ones you love so they never have to experience moral atrocity? I was powerless to do anything but squeeze Burke tighter.

Sheriff Marge's next question was quiet, and felt like an afterthought, although it clearly wasn't. "Did they see you?"

Burke took a long time to answer. "I don't think so."

"But you're not sure?"

He shook his head. "The bossy guy was sure staring, right at the spot where I was hiding. Some of the bushes lose their leaves in the winter. I couldn't be sure he didn't see me through the branches."

That's when I knew. It wasn't hunger or loneliness that had driven Burke to set out on his own, to abandon the cabin he called home, the place where he'd promised to serve as caretaker for his beloved father.

He was afraid for his life.

CHAPTER 13

Sheriff Marge's phone rang, jolting me past that paralyzing realization. She snuck a glance at the caller ID and pushed to her feet. "Gotta take this," she grunted, and ambled out into the hallway, the equipment on her duty belt jutting out around her broad hips.

I angled an arm around Burke and pressed the stop button on the recorder. The silence in the room was oppressive, interrupted only by the whooshing ticks of the refrigerator's compressor. I felt like I was encased in resin—inert, ineffective, a prime specimen of the aftermath of catastrophe, preserved for future generations to marvel over, a warning to take heed while they still had life in their veins.

Pete reached out and ruffled Burke's hair. "I heard you were helping Mr. Hagg clean his office."

The look on Burke's face was priceless—and so incongruous with our current situation that I nearly burst into tears. Happy tears, relieved tears, I think, but my emotional barometer had been haywire lately.

Because his grin was a blast of sunshine in the gloomy room. We hadn't turned on the overhead lights, instead relying on the daylight filtering in through the window. But that source of illumination was rapidly dwindling, and I noted new white specs floating down from the pewter-bellied clouds outside.

"More like tunneling," Burke giggled.

Actually giggled. Like a kid.

Pete locked jubilant gazes with me for a second, then said, "I suppose you could go back upstairs and help him some more. We'll head home in a bit, though."

And just like that, Burke slid off my lap and made a beeline for the door. Just like a normal kid.

I stared at Pete.

"For everybody's mental health," he murmured. "If Sheriff Marge needs more information, we can go over the facts again tomorrow. But right now..." He clapped a hand on the back of his neck and shook his head slowly.

"Do you need to be held, too?" I whispered.

He opened his arms to me, the tiniest sparkle returning to his gorgeous sapphire-blue eyes, and I clambered aboard.

"This isn't quite the same thing," I objected, nestling into his shoulder with absolutely no intention of actually reversing roles.

"Still does the trick," he murmured against my neck.

His hands were roaming proprietarily, and I squirmed against him. "I'm sorry," I whispered. "So sorry—for all of this."

"I know, babe. We all are. We'll make it as right as we can for Burke."

~oOo~

We found Sheriff Marge in the ballroom, standing with her hands on her hips, glaring out through the double glass doors at the fairy dust snow that was starting to skim across the tire tracks in the parking lot, seemingly lost in her own thoughts.

But she must've heard us coming, because her first words were directed at our reflections in the glass as well as at the inclement weather on the other side. "I know who she is."

"That was fast," I replied. "The medical examiner's already—?"

"Nope." She hitched up her duty belt and continued glaring at the frigid dandruff outside. "She matches a missing person report out of Whitman County. That was Sheriff McNary on the line. He's missing one university student who was reported absent by her fellow research assistants four days ago. Not too many twenty-seven-year-old blonde female doctoral candidates with a titanium knee bumbling around these parts. Looks like she got herself into a bad situation."

"You think she's to blame?" I whispered.

"No." Sheriff Marge lifted her glasses with a finger and pinched the bridge of her nose. "No, I don't. Didn't mean it to come out that way. It's just that if our corpse really is Ms. Cassidy Kendall, then there's a huge gap in her time line—longer than the four days anyone's known about it, because the early reports are that she was last seen nearly two weeks ago, and I've got next to nothing to work with for an investigation." She resettled the glasses and turned to pierce me with those steel-gray eyes. "Except our boy's eyewitness testimony."

"Meaning you're worried about his safety," Pete said.

Sheriff Marge's lips flattened into a thin, pinched line. "His unusual circumstances, and the fact that he showed up out of the blue, have already generated some buzz in the community. Add to that the fact that it's hard to keep an all-hands search on Gifford Mountain a true secret. Even harder to keep finding a murder victim under wraps. If those two men tap into the rumor pipeline and put two and two together, well..." She shook her head. "Given the vicious nature of the crime, I have no doubt they'd follow up in a similar vein if they thought it necessary."

"So we have to keep him hidden, out of the way..." I glanced around the festive ballroom frothy with bunting in Val's chosen colors of pale, icy blue and silver, with its glittering accents, and a long buffet table set with the stainless steel bases for chafing dishes and coffee service. All that was missing was a disco ball, but even we're not so redneck as all that.

The setting was so incongruous—the trappings of the highly anticipated celebration all around us compared to the stark depravity we'd just been discussing. And how to mask the presence of a small boy in the midst of all this?

Strength in numbers? In Sockeye County, where every single one of those numbers had eyes peeled for anything out of the ordinary—just as Sheriff Marge had pointed out—I wasn't so sure. But it wasn't like we were going to lock him in a closet, either.

I shuddered again, and it shook something loose. Or maybe I just wanted the distraction, but for some reason, the color scheme floating around me in gauzy layers reminded me of the titanium knee. "She was awfully young for a knee replacement," I murmured.

"Volleyball," Sheriff Marge grunted.

I squinted at her.

"Star volleyball player for her high school team. Homecoming queen. All-around girl-next-door and sweetheart of the one-light town of Garfield, Washington. Recruited by the *big leagues*"—Sheriff Marge put air quotes around the term with her knuckly fingers— "of women's college volleyball programs. Stanford, the Universities of Texas, Nebraska, Kansas. She had her pick, and then her knee blew out in a pick-up game the day after graduation. Extensive surgery sidelined her for a year, and she postponed college to focus on her recovery. Then a motorcycle accident nearly tore off that same knee six months later. Required a full replacement, but they did manage to save her leg. Apparently the other option was amputation. The whole town—no, the whole county—knows her history. Sheriff McNary spent ten minutes reciting it to me."

It sounded just like Platts Landing—this small community of Garfield. Even though I'd never been there, I could instantly picture it all, how vested the few hundred residents would be in the prospects of their shining star, how much pressure she must've been under. To have it all wrecked through a series of unfortunate accidents.

Pete knew too. He'd had a similar situation with one of his knees. Not so extreme, but it still ruined his prospects for a football-scholarship-paid college education. So he'd chosen the Navy. "So she stayed close to home?" he asked.

"Right." Sheriff Marge nodded. "Smart girl. She got a partial scholarship on her academic merit and ended up at Washington State University in Pullman. Flying right through all their programs—bachelor's, master's, now doctoral. Apparently, she's quite the research phenom. Majoring in Environmental Sciences, with a specialty in grain crops."

"Well, she's in the right place, then," Pete agreed with somber satisfaction. But then he winced. "Or *was*. All the farmers and co-ops I tow grain barges for rely on the research coming out of WSU to increase their yields and the grade of their crops. A tiny improvement can have a huge impact on their bottom line because of the sheer acreage involved."

"Do you think she was targeted? Or selected at random?" The words were barely out of my mouth when I remembered that Burke had said the men and Cassidy—it was both weird and strangely comforting to attach a real name to the image of the damaged woman in my mind—had been chatting amicably just before the men's sudden change in intent became apparent. Not a likely scenario between a kidnappee and her abductors. So the answer was *targeted*. But what if they'd decided on the spur of the moment? What if their orchestrated actions had been rehearsed? Or implemented previously? Maybe they were a serial killer duo, and specialized in grooming their victims ahead of time, in gaining their trust.

I jerked my thoughts away from that line of unreasonable and macabre speculation and added quickly, "Because if there's a lot of money involved with what Cassidy was researching, then...?" I shrugged to fill in the blank.

"She was a beautiful—and from all reports, personable—young woman," Sheriff Marge growled. "There's a huge spectrum of possible motives, and the methods also could vary from opportunistic to intricately plotted." She heaved a sigh. "I have my work cut out for me."

I wanted so desperately to wrap her in a hug. Not that it would solve her problems. And probably more for my own sake than for hers, but Sheriff Marge isn't a woman who receives hugs gladly. For one thing, all that equipment and the ballistic vest make it awkward, but I knew from experience that when in crime-solving mode— as opposed to her usual mother-hen mode, and the transformational process was occurring before my very eyes—she became more aloof, more reserved, more focused. In all her iterations, she's a formidable woman, and I'd do anything I could to help her.

But what to offer?

It turned out I didn't need to blurt out any bumbling suggestions, because Sheriff Marge knew exactly what to do next. "I'm going to have the high school art teacher come out to your place tonight. She serves as my sketch artist when the need arises. She'll sit with Burke and get us some drawings of the two men to work from."

"Of course," Pete responded. "But what about Burke? What did you find in the cabin? Is there anything we should be aware of in our interactions with him—about the murder, or about his past, his father?"

We were clearly out of our depth in this new foster-parenting role, and I was so grateful Pete had asked that hard, open-ended question. I sidled over to him and slipped my hand into his.

Sheriff Marge returned to pinching the bridge of her nose as though a migraine was setting in. "I still have calls out about that—to confirm things," she replied. "But the early analysis indicates he was a university professor who was denied tenure under a great deal of contention. There was some paperwork in the cabin with Oregon State University's logo on it which I skimmed through. Basically, he was fired—as fired as you can get in academia without having violated ethics regulations, at any rate. It seems he was sticking to his guns about a research tangent that the college dean didn't approve of. Something the school didn't want pursued. My guess is it was a messy political situation, probably grudges born on each side, possibly a crushed reputation. At any rate, it was sufficiently devastating that Professor Brightbill took his son and disappeared into no-man's land."

Pete and I were silent for a long minute, letting the information sink in, my shoulder rubbing against his arm with each breath. Then, as though reading my mind, Pete said, "So Burke's dad was fired for abiding by his conscience in a professional matter?"

"That's the gist of it."

"And his mom?" I whispered. "Any hints about her?"

"Ah." Sheriff Marge seemed to deflate even further under her gear. "Found that too. Cullen Brightbill kept organized files, even while living in the boonies. A copy of a death certificate. Four years ago. Ovarian cancer."

Layer upon layer of loss. I turned my face into Pete's shoulder, and he cupped his hand around the back of my head.

"I hate saying this," Sheriff Marge continued, "but this actually makes Burke's situation easier from a red-tape perspective because with these documents we have proof that he's truly an orphan and truly a ward of Washington State. And therefore truly yours, for the time being. I'm not stretching my authority on that subject anymore. You've heard from Hester?"

I nodded. "We have an interview appointment set for Monday evening. She's coming out to check the house, verify that Burke'll have a bedroom of his own, that we can feed him, stuff like that. She said she'd talk us through the training process, see what parts of it we could speed up."

"Good, good." Sheriff Marge drew a deep breath and shoved her hat back on her forehead. "Best news I've had all day. I suspect our boy holds himself responsible for some of what he saw, if not all of it, and is thinking he should've prevented it in some way. He's going to need to talk about it—in his own time—and he'll need you to help him process. I can't think of a better couple to handle this than the two of you."

CHAPTER 14

The weight of the world. No, scratch that. The weight of the sin in the world. Which is greater. Much, much greater. Snatches of some of Pastor Mort's recent sermons strung themselves together in my brain, reminding me again of how ill-equipped I am to handle this stuff on my own, and of the power of grace. How we need grace. Right now. In this very moment.

It came in the form of Frankie's head, popped around the corner from the gift shop. And then the rest of her efficient, organized, bustling form in short order. A big clump of keys jangled in her hand.

"Locking up for the night," she announced, darting glances from my face to Pete's to Sheriff Marge's and back again. "Uh-oh," she said. "Tell me. You have to tell me." She quickly strode to my side and squeezed my free hand with liberal commiseration. "What is it?"

But she kept talking, filling in our reluctant silence. "It's the young woman, isn't it? Henry told me...some. Why did they leave her—just—exposed like that?" she finished in a rasping whisper.

We were the recipients of one of Sheriff Marge's long, drawn-out, scrutinizing gazes, as though she were testing us for leaks. After a moment, she decided and repositioned her hands on her hips. "I have a hypothesis about that as well. Didn't want to tell you, actually, even though it's all the more reason for us to keep Burke sequestered."

"Oh dear," Frankie breathed beside me. "Oh dear."

I wanted to give Sheriff Marge a piece of my mind for not confiding fully in us, but what authority did I have? She was just taking her serve-and-protect role seriously, as always. So I stared at her instead, breath frozen in my chest.

"This murder was either luckily nearly perfect, or the perpetrators were uncannily clever. I don't know which yet." Sheriff Marge pulled one of the rented folding chairs that had been draped over the back with a huge silver bow out from under the long skirt of a pale blue tablecloth and dropped onto it. "Sit..." She gestured wearily. "Mac and Val won't mind."

Which was true. If we were careful, they'd never know we'd used their reception hall for such a stomach-roiling conversation. The rest of us quickly scrabbled into chairs of our own, and Pete shoved the exuberant centerpiece out of the way so we could all see each other clearly in the sparkly, romantic glow of the twinkle lights.

"First of all," Sheriff Marge said, "they left Cassidy exposed to the elements precisely so that the process that had begun would continue to completion, namely the natural order of things."

Which still wasn't entirely obvious to me. I had my mouth open to request clarification, but Pete beat me to it.

He had to clear his throat to do so. "You mean being eaten by wild animals."

I'd forgotten—already. He'd seen Cassidy's body—with all that entailed. I pressed my hands between my thighs to keep them from trembling.

Sheriff Marge nodded slowly. "Yes, and the decay process. Decomposition has a predictable sequence and time line, but there are a few factors that'll either slow it down or speed it up. Ambient temperature and submersion, either in soil or water, are the two most important variables. Cassidy's killers seemed to know this. By removing some of her clothing, they accomplished several things. One, the body would cool faster, thus slowing her decay rate. That would be a negative from their perspective. But they exposed more of her flesh to the elements, which successfully attracted the wild animals. Also, people suffering from hypothermia often get confused and misread the signals their body is sending them and they'll remove their own clothing, thinking they're hot instead of cold."

Pete tensed. I felt it like an electrical charge across the foot or so of air space that separated us. His leg was bouncing rapidly under the table. "They were trying to make it look like an accident."

"They were very careful," Sheriff Marge hedged. "When I hear back from the ME, I expect he's going to tell me she had no broken bones. There might be some scrapes on a vertebrae or two in her neck from the rope noose, but they'll be minor and would've been inconclusive once her soft flesh was completely gone."

Frankie moaned quietly.

"If we'd found her body when it was a more likely situation—say in March or April when the mushroom hunters start wandering around in the hills—we wouldn't have been able to pinpoint her cause of death. It could've been any number of things—hypothermia, as I mentioned already; maybe a fall that wrenched her neck; or a traumatic subdural hematoma from hitting her head on rocks. Murder would've been much harder, if not impossible, to prove. Burying her would've made it obvious her death was intentional." Sheriff Marge shrugged. "Not to mention the ground up there is incredibly rocky and frozen. Impractical for a number of reasons."

"So the only flaw in their plan is one little boy," I murmured.

"Exactly."

"Which they may or may not know about," Frankie amended, with a trace of optimism in her hushed tone.

~oOo~

Rupert shocked me with the speed with which he soft-shoed down the staircase and just about tumbled, roly-poly like, into the ballroom. His pace was possibly explained by the fact that he was hard on the heels of a thundering eleven-year-old boy.

It was an instant dilemma. Did we all jump to our feet and pretend we hadn't been embroiled in a serious, adults-only—and therefore intriguing—conversation, or did we lounge resolutely in those gaudily decorated chairs and aim for the impression that we'd just been shooting the breeze in a lazy fashion? Neither option was fantastic or in line with our normal behavior, but we all stayed glued to our seats as though by mutual agreement.

"Well," Rupert huffed, squinting around at our melancholy faces. "No success. Those Pinkerton items are proving elusive. I'm beginning to doubt their very existence, except as figments of my imagination."

I scowled at him. What was he suggesting?

He was returning my glower right back, as though trying to divine the reason for the somber mood in our little cluster. I'd give him one out of three guesses, but it was obvious from his pitched brow and short, puffed exhale that he needn't have guessed at all. He knew.

"So," he continued without the slightest hesitation, "I propose a continuance. Tomorrow, perhaps? I, myself, find wedding receptions rather boring and dull affairs. If Burke—" Rupert aimed a short bow in the boy's direction—"would honor me with the pleasure of his company and nimble limbs for furthering the search tomorrow afternoon, I would be tremendously grateful. With your approval, of course."

And just like that Rupert solved our primary problem—how to keep Burke hidden during a mass community event. I gasped with relief, then realized he was eyeing me expectantly. What had he asked? Permission?

Oh, right, the parental thing to do. Burke, too, was watching me with eager, if subdued, delight. How could I possibly deny these two boys—one old, one young—their treasure hunt?

I nodded quickly. "Sounds like a plan."

"Humph," Frankie reminded me.

She was right. The minor alteration in arrangements meant we'd have to postpone our matchmaking efforts where Rupert was concerned. But the current need was far, far greater.

~oOo~

The sketch artist was a delight. Ms. Olivia Oliphant.

And if her name made me want to giggle, then her appearance exacerbated that particularly inappropriate social response to the point of nearly bursting. But her ready smile, in spite of the circumstances—complete with crooked, feathered neon-pink lipstick—was incredibly endearing. And alarming. But mostly endearing.

She also knew to knock on the kitchen door instead of the front door. My kind of people.

"Come in," I urged, stepping back to allow her to pass. She brought in a slurry of melting snowflakes with her—they were clinging in slushy clumps to her thick faux-leopard, faux-fur, knee-length, uh...robe. It wasn't a coat, per se. More like a heaping swirl of mangy fabric that she'd swathed herself in. How she managed to be ambulatory, let alone drive, while so encumbered, I couldn't even begin to guess.

But she was certainly walking—and talking. Nonstop.

And she knew Pete. Had to stand up on her tippy toes—in bright-green, four-inch-heel, Mary Jane pumps, no less—to wrap her knobbed, arthritic fingers around the back of his neck and pull him down for a loud smackeroo on the cheek.

"Oh, you!" she gushed. "I knew you'd grow up to be a handsome devil. Such a time you gave me in class! That stunt with the rubber cement and the toothpicks and the Vaseline, ooch! And then that incident with the glow-in-the-dark tempera paint and the skeleton from Mr. Foster's biology lab." She clucked chidingly and shed her robe into a heap on the floor.

I picked it up and hung it to drip neatly on a peg by the door. Then I dampened a paper towel at the sink and handed it to Pete with a pointed look at the long neon-pink smear along the edge of his jaw. He was still chuckling, and an embarrassed (and absolutely adorable, although I would never say so) flush had crept up his neck. He was going to be grilled—thoroughly grilled—about his high school shenanigans later, and I think he knew it.

Ms. Oliphant had slung her monstrous bag—apparently handknit of some kind of shredded sea grass with wooden beads painted like ladybugs interspersed in the design—onto the kitchen table, and she was now pawing through its cavernous interior. "I'll just be getting my graphite sticks out, and a pad of newsprint. I understand time is of the essence, but I couldn't get out here any sooner because Laddie—my dog, you know—has indigestion, and he has to be watched after he's fed for a certain length of time, otherwise I come back to a disastrous mess in the house. Poor dog. Unlike your sweet hound here. She's a shy one, isn't she?"

Tuppence was cowering under the table, pressed hard against Burke's legs. Burke almost looked as though he'd like to slide under that protective surface and join my dog. Olivia Oliphant had a commandeering presence—the kind of personality that might be able to swallow small children whole. But Pete had survived.

"How about the living room?" I suggested loudly over Ms. Oliphant's continued running commentary. "I'll bring you some tea."

"Oh, lovely, dear. Lovely, lovely, lovely." And she began wandering toward the nearest doorway, clutching an armful of supplies to her chest.

Pete snagged her elbow just before she began descending into the basement and redirected her toward the front room with the comfortable sofas and padded armchairs.

"Oh, this way? Silly me. Seems the last time I was in this house, Harriet had the living room down there. Or maybe it was her sewing room. Did you know she helped me with the costumes for the eighth-grade presentation of *Oklahoma!*? That was before I put my foot down and told the school board I could handle only so much nonsense in one school year, and they agreed to switch me to teaching high school art classes only. That young gal they hired for the younger grades lasted just one year, bless her heart. Wimpy, just wasn't cut out for the rigors of education, that one. Crashed and burned, poor dear..." The clarity of her words petered out as she rounded the corner, even though the general air of constant blather remained swirling like little dust devils in the kitchen.

Burke and I blinked at each other, just trying to regain our bearings, I think.

"Well," I murmured into the static leftover from Ms. Oliphant's monologue.

A slow grin spread, and nearly cracked his face in half. Those mineral-green eyes shimmered like iridescent pools in a deep forest.

"Think you can handle this?" I asked.

He nodded—even eagerly, it seemed.

"Off you go, then."

Tuppence stuck to his heels as though he offered some kind of magic protection from the startlingly flamboyant woman who'd invaded the house, and they slid into the living room together. I set about performing my hostess duties as quickly as possible. In truth, I didn't want to miss a minute of the sketching process. And Burke would need backup—maybe.

But when I carried in a tray of tea things, Burke, to my immense surprise, was wedged in next to Ms. Oliphant on the sofa and was answering her soft questions with murmurs and short shifts of his head—up and down, or side to side. He was close enough that his cheek occasionally brushed her sleeve. She also had toned down her chatter, and they were both deeply absorbed in whatever was manifesting underneath the deft strokes of her graphite sticks.

From Pete's intense blue glance, I could tell he was impressed. He'd stationed himself just over their shoulders, watching unobtrusively, and I went to join him.

"Do you know him?" I breathed after a few minutes, when the solid chin and sharp nose with flared nostrils of what I assumed was the larger of the two murderers took on a more defined shape.

Beside me, Pete shook his head.

The result was the same for the second drawing, of the smaller, bossy man. Very clear, very distinct features—but none of us recognized either one.

"You're sure, Burke?" Ms. Oliphant asked. Without waiting for an answer, she heaved herself off the sofa and strode to the far wall, spun around and held up one drawing in each hand, her arms spread wide. "How about from a distance? I can change anything you want."

Her thick, murky opaque taupe stockings—manufactured of a yarn denier more common prior to WWII—bagged around her ankles, and her hair—what I now realized was of the faux-extension variety—was clumped unattractively over one ear, but she'd achieved wizardry with the drawings. The two men seemed poised to lunge off the newsprint, the menacing scowls on their faces making my heart thump faster than normal.

I grabbed Pete's hand, and he gave me a reassuring squeeze.

"That's them," Burke answered quietly, but firmly.

While she sipped her tea, Ms. Oliphant transferred her sketches to larger sheets of watercolor paper.

"People don't think in black and white anymore," she lamented. "Not since the movies switched over to Technicolor. You have to feed a likeness to them—hook, line, and sinker. Otherwise this bozo could walk right by and they'd never make the connection."

I was a little worried about what direction her comments would start to run toward now that her focus had a little more leeway, so I sent Burke upstairs to take a bath. He obeyed, but with a foot-dragging reluctance that would've made me chuckle—and probably relent—under other circumstances.

"Do this often?" I asked when he was safely out of earshot.

Ms. Oliphant shook her head, the tip of her tongue pointing doggedly out of the corner of her mouth as she swabbed in the first smear of pale blue paint. "More often than anyone would like. First time the witness has been so young, though," she added in a hoarse whisper. "Poor mite."

"He seemed to do okay," I added in my own whisper, more to reassure myself than anything. "He provided an extraordinary amount of detail." I wasn't sure what I'd been expecting, but the drawings were rendered with a clarity that was still disturbing me.

"Oh, yes." Ms. Oliphant fixed me with a cloudy stare. Cataracts obscured her eye color to the point of making it unidentifiable, and I wondered how she could produce such accurate sketches—and now paintings. "He's a brilliant child," she said approvingly. "Sheriff Marge gave me a bit of background—all part of explaining the urgency, you see. Since Burke hasn't been distracted by television or video games or any of that other nonsense children are subjected to these days, he's marvelously astute." She returned to swishing paints around on the paper. "When you live in nature, you necessarily learn to observe extensively—out of self-preservation and, in his case it seems, innate curiosity as well. He'll be a fine young man."

I figured her predictive powers were pretty accurate. I grinned up at Pete. Because she'd made the right call on him too.

CHAPTER 15

The next day—Saturday—was like a blast of incredibly chilly fresh air. Because it was a blast of incredibly chilly fresh air. Fortunately the air didn't come with much precipitation in it, although the white stuff that was already on the ground stayed there, sparkling like crystallized frosting on every surface and still clinging to the bare oak branches and the evergreen boughs of the trees in the county park that surrounds the Imogene Museum.

With the silvery-gray expanse of the river flowing beside the mansion and the powder dusted hills on the Oregon side, the setting couldn't have been a more spectacular backdrop for a wedding reception. Particularly for the out-of-towners who don't take our marvelous scenery for granted. The wedding party smiled gallantly while their lips turned blue and the photographer dictated poses and positions for picture after picture after picture.

She'd come prepared—in a down parka with fur rimming the hood and fingerless gloves so she could still flip the little switches and press the shutter buttons on her bevy of cameras. But I felt terrible for the poor bridesmaids in their shimmering, silky, sleeveless gowns and strappy sandals. Those girls were going to need heated benches like NFL players get in Green Bay, or at the very least, warm blankets—which Frankie, bless her heart, thought of and popped in to roast on low in the museum's kitchen oven.

The rest of Mac and Val's guests streamed through the Imogene's front doors, their breath frozen and suspended in front of their mouths like hesitant ghosts, and the ballroom was soon buzzing with the cheerful screeches of long-lost friends greeting one another, general back slapping, and chair legs scraping on the floor as people found their place cards and took up battle stations for the festivities to come. There was also a run on the restrooms.

Pete and I had entrusted Burke to Rupert's care, and the two of them had skedaddled out of the back of the church on the coattails of the wedding party. I'm pretty sure that if anyone noticed a small-for-his-age boy with giant blue-green eyes flitting like a waif in the foyer, they all assumed he was the offspring of one of the many visiting guests and didn't give him a second thought. At least that was what I was hoping, with my fingers crossed, while I thought of him safely ensconced up on the third floor in Rupert's time capsule-slash-office. I'd take some food to them later and check to make sure they hadn't been buried under an avalanche of items of historical and sentimental value.

For the moment, I was the girl with the clipboard, a little too much like a Frankie clone for my comfort, but nonetheless stationed just inside the double glass doors at her bidding and pointing guests in the general direction of their assigned seats. We figured they could read the diagram, but they still might need a little help getting their bearings and navigating through the large room.

Deputy Owen Hobart, looking mighty spiffy in his khaki uniform—whether he was on duty or not, I wasn't sure, but with all the starch and buttons the uniform still might've been the nicest suit of clothes he owned—stepped through the doorway, his brown eyes raking the room with a dazed sort of overwhelmedness in his expression. This event was a pretty far cry from his usual search and rescue and patrol responsibilities, and I felt a pang of empathy for him. Maybe all the formality was a touch claustrophobic for him.

"Hey, Owen," I murmured. "Thanks for...well, Pete told me, uh...some." I wrinkled my nose at my own awkwardness. I was supposed to be helping the guests, not confusing them in the doorway. But I couldn't say a whole lot about what I wanted to say—if you get my meaning.

Owen certainly did. "Yeah, sure." He flashed me a quick glance along with a nod. "Just doing my duty. We'll get it sorted."

I had no doubt they would. All of them—Sheriff Marge and her three deputies. Even if they worked a hundred hours a week each for the next three months, they wouldn't stop until they'd *sorted* the problem on Gifford Mountain.

The problem was, I wasn't sure we—meaning Burke especially—had the luxury of the time it would take the severely undermanned sheriff's department to complete the task and bring the murderers to justice. There were just so many loose ends, so many unknowns. They were faced with a research project of epic proportions, and when I thought about it that way, I could certainly relate, my knees nearly buckling with the magnitude of the job before them.

But I pointed Owen toward a table in the front corner of the room and suggested he could be on warm-blanket duty when the wedding party was released from smiling for the camera since there was a lovely bridesmaid assigned to the same table with him.

He pinked up in a way that had nothing to do with the brisk temperature outside and slipped into the gathering throng, edging around the perimeter of the room like a border collie keeping tabs on all his sheep— just watching, ever alert.

~oOo~

Mac MacDougal—the groom—was acting as his own master of ceremonies. I suppose that's taboo normally, but in Sockeye County the rules of etiquette are what you make them, and Mac was bringing the house down. It may have been an innate bartender skill, or it may have just been Mac himself—the guy is indefatigable, and utterly charming in an inexcusably corny way. Especially now that he's married to someone else.

And his new bride was thoroughly enjoying his banter, laughing and blushing furiously, cheering when it was warranted, and occasionally looking as though she might want to disappear under the head table with her dog, Rosie, who was dressed prettily with a big blue bow on her collar and who'd acted as ring bearer during the ceremony. But I couldn't have been happier for Val, and, all things considered, she'd definitely known what she was getting into. I caught her eye from across the room, and she gave me a happy little wave.

I was rather enjoying the fact that as hostess/organizer/person-in-charge under Frankie, I wasn't assigned to a table myself. So I got to wander and watch and dart in and out and hopefully avert any disasters in the making. Of which there were only a few. Mostly I got to eavesdrop.

After the obligatory oohing and ahhing over the decorations and the lights and the glamor of the ceremony and all the usual things people say about weddings, most of the celebrants settled down to the serious business of eating while rehashing community goings-on of note. Which turned out to be primarily the spree of petty thefts and vandalism that seemed to have affected—directly or indirectly—just about everyone.

Someone—or a set of someones, connected or not, no one was sure, although there was rampant speculation—was making their mark on the county. Quite literally, in the form of spray paint and broken windows and cut chain-link fences and slashed tires, a few stolen vehicles, etcetera. The perpetrators were creative, to be sure, and had garnered the attention of the entire county. No wonder Sheriff Marge was fit to be tied. No wonder she was stretched to the point of breaking, trying to handle all those complaints plus a murder investigation. And no wonder she also had a burr under her saddle about the new exhibit.

Any little thing that could help slow the rate of crime in the county would give her a much-needed boost. I silently vowed to redouble my efforts along the cultural awareness and solidarity front that the Imogene and all her treasures on display represents, particularly in the form of the new exhibit. She wasn't going to like the fact that the rumor mill had so enthusiastically grabbed ahold of the petty crimes, but the alternative—that the community at large knew enough about the murder to speculate upon it as well—was worse. So far, it seemed that knowledge of the much direr situation had been contained to a narrow group of people. I needed to do everything I could to keep it that way.

Pete, handsome in the charcoal-gray suit and jaunty bow tie dictated upon groomsmen, found me lurking in the corner behind the towering wedding cake and wrapped his arms around my waist from behind, snugging me up against his chest. "Glad we're finished with all the pomp and hoopla, babe?" he murmured into my ear. "Settled-down is good, yeah?"

I nodded vigorously and leaned against him, reveling in his warmth. "We narrowly escaped. I couldn't imagine having a bash like this."

"How's the kid?" he whispered even more quietly, his seven-o'clock shadow scritching against my cheek.

"I took them plates of food about half an hour ago. Neither Rupert nor Burke did more than holler that they were okay from somewhere deep in the stacks. The fact that they didn't immediately come out and ravenously scarf the food means they're hot on the trail of something good up there." I chuckled. "In other words, he's fine. If rubble and mass disorganization are defense mechanisms, then Rupert's office is the safest place in the world for him."

"The mood's pretty somber—for all the happiness," Pete said, jutting his chin toward the guests. "You'd think people would be giddy for finally having succeeded in getting Mac and Val to tie the knot, but they're already on to grumbling about the latest problem."

I nodded again. "About the crime wave? They're worried. I don't blame them. Sounds like it's affected most of the retail businesses in Platts Landing and many in Lupine as well," I added, mentioning the county seat about twenty minutes to the east, and the heart of Sheriff Marge's jurisdiction.

Pete angled me to the side so he could look into my face. "Crime wave?"

I frowned. We'd both been mingling through the crowd, so clearly our eavesdropping radar were tuned differently—if we'd been hearing, and registering, different topics. "What's your subject du jour?" I asked, suddenly anxious that maybe some people *were* spreading the word about the murder.

"SeedGenix."

"Ohhh," I murmured, and exhaled with relief. The major supplier of crop seed for the farmers in the region. The company specialized in developing strains that flourish on the irrigated plateaus that flank the Columbia River throughout the watershed basin. The name of the company was both a blessing and a curse, depending on who was saying it and at what point we were in the planting/growing/harvesting cycle.

Of course Pete would pay attention to those conversations because the resulting wheat, corn, and soybeans constituted the majority of his tows for the months of August through November each year. And in the spring when the river's lock system reopened after winter maintenance, he'd pick up the grain reserves from the various co-op elevators and get those to market as well. That was the way the farmers hedged some of their bets—holding a portion of their harvest back while waiting to see what happened to commodity prices. A tight interplay of percentages and risk, feast and famine.

When the crops performed well, so did Pete—as measured by bushels, short tons, and cubic feet. I know some of the lingo just from hanging around my hubby, but the sheer volume of the annual grain shipments is still unfathomable to my mind.

"They're not getting the rebates they were promised," Pete said.

He must have noticed the blank expression on my face, because he pulled me around the cake table and out onto the dance floor. The band had just struck up a lilting melody with a soft beat that it seemed even I might be able to shuffle to.

"It's a tactic SeedGenix has been taking the past few years to try to beat out their competitors. They sell their seeds at the same price as the two other big seed companies from the Midwest—it's not like the farmers have a lot of choices about who to buy their seed from. But SeedGenix has been offering rebates to the farmers based on germination rate." Pete finagled my hand up onto his shoulder and grasped my other one in his, while his hand on my back told me where to go.

How he could talk and keep the rhythm with his steps at the same time, I'll never know. Inside my head, I was counting silently but still lurched about in belated syncopated fashion. "Explain that to me," I breathed quickly between steps 2 and 3 on the little chart in my head.

It was a little challenge. I was waiting to see if he could do it—manage a layman's explanation of the complicated regional economics and foxtrot simultaneously. I needn't have bothered. Piece of cake, apparently—and figuratively, since the newlyweds had yet to cut the real one.

"When the winter wheat went in this fall, the SeedGenix salesmen promised rebates to the farmers based on the germination rate. Eighty percent is industry standard. So they set up a directly correlated rebate—for every percentage point over eighty, they also offered a matching percentage off the farmer's total seed bill. A lot of those guys have to finance their seed buy and then make monthly payments, so to have that total decrease, even by a few percentage points, would be huge for them. Win-win."

I tipped my chin against Pete's shoulder and scowled at nobody in particular. Because that didn't make sense to me. But maybe there was an error in my math. Could be my fancy footwork was diverting blood flow from my brain. "I don't understand," I replied. "Isn't that win-lose? If SeedGenix produces an amazing wheat seed that germinates more than usual, therefore yielding more per acre, but the farmer has to pay less for that seed because of this very same amazing capability—then the farmer saves money with the rebate while the company loses profit after they spent a lot of time and effort on research and development." I leaned back to gaze into his crinkle-cornered eyes.

To find he was grinning down at me. "I was just giving you the sales spiel. Word for word what the SeedGenix salesmen were promising the farmers."

I snorted. "Those salesmen need to have their heads examined." And then another thought hit me. "Did the farmers get the offers in writing?" Because this was sounding hinky. Like ulterior-motive hinky. I'd known some big talkers in my time, some high-pressure sales-types. I'd even been engaged to one once, although he'd been disguised as a lawyer. The personality was identical, though. And if those salesmen were under pressure of their own from upper management, I wouldn't be surprised if they manufactured off-the-books deals in order to meet their completely arbitrary quotas.

"But the opposite is true as well. If the seed underperformed, the farmers wouldn't have gotten any discount, and the company would've kept the full purchase price, thereby profiting more. So that would be a reverse incentive for the company—lose-win." I shook my head with the confusion of the concept.

"Hence the grumbling," Pete said. "The farmers are in a tight spot regardless because SeedGenix has what amounts to a stranglehold on the supply. *And* they're the ones who verify the germination rates."

My blood was rising, too, just thinking about it. "That stinks. There should be third-party verification."

"Indeed."

I began to wonder if all the murmurings Pete and I had been hearing were, in fact, related. Because problems at the top of the socio-economic ladder filter down very quickly in a place like Sockeye County. There just aren't that many rungs.

CHAPTER 16

Hot damn he thought again—for about the millionth time—his vocabulary having shrunk noticeably. Whatever words had been in his brain half a second ago had vaporized. Also, his tongue was sticking to the roof of his mouth. If he did manage to actually open his trap, something that sounded suspiciously like *aargh aargh grunt aargh* would probably come out. Nothing suave, that was for sure.

So he studied the remains of the prime rib dinner on his plate. He hadn't devoured the meal with remarkable efficiency, the way he normally ate, because he didn't want to gross out the girl sitting next to him. The girl all the silent *hot damns* were for. Darcy—Darcy O'Hare she'd said her name was.

And then she hadn't spoken to him again, either. Probably wishing she'd been assigned to any other table but this one—with a bunch of geriatrics and a stone-cold silent, boring galoot of a deputy sheriff who probably hadn't used his knife properly while cutting the meat. Not such a fun night for a single girl.

Hot damn, but she was all dimples and curves in that clingy, silky bridesmaid dress. And huge blue eyes with flawless, creamy skin—he could see quite a lot of her skin, actually, because of the dress. But it was her deep, coppery red hair with golden sparkles in it that was really doing him in. He was staring—he knew he was staring, so once more, he quickly averted his gaze to the congealed gravy smears on his plate.

Maybe he could've talked, if he'd had a subject that wasn't off-limits. But all he did was work, and telling a pretty girl about finding the murdered body of a different pretty girl wasn't a good idea. He supposed he could brag about how fast his patrol car could go or that one time he cold-cocked a scrawny teenage robber who was running out of a 7-Eleven. But that was just a case of being in the right place at the right time, since he'd been going inside to get himself a Slurpee, so he could hardly take credit for it.

Hot damn, but she had amazing eyelashes too. Even they were curvy, and long. He was staring again, enough to make her blush. He cleared his throat, opened his mouth, closed it.

Why wasn't she a chatterbox? Most girls were. He'd been in several situations with girls where they seemed to happily fill in all the blanks in the conversation, so he'd had to say very little at all. Easy. They'd made it easy.

Darcy wasn't making it easy. He sort of liked her better for it, though—if that was possible. But it'd be up to him...

He cleared his throat again, shuffled his big feet under the table. Finally the band launched into a song that seemed the right tempo. Not crazy fast, but not so slow that the only option was super-close dancing. Just right. Maybe.

He coiled up every ounce of nerve he had and briefly—just for a fleeting nanosecond—skimmed a fingertip on her gorgeous bare arm. "Would you like to dance?" It came out like a croak. Like a frog with laryngitis.

She beamed at him, and he just about fell off his chair.

And then she gave him her whole hand, and he wasn't quite sure what to do with it. Except, well, hold it, and stand up—and she rose with him, every curvy inch of her, and she dropped her napkin on the table next to her plate. *HOT DAMN.*

His legs were wobbly, but he made it to the dance floor, and then she was in his arms and she smelled heavenly, and he wasn't sure if his feet were moving or not, but he wasn't sure if it mattered either.

~oOo~

"Will you look at that." Frankie's tone was ripe with satisfaction, her hands clasped tightly together at her waist, almost as though she was restraining a victory jig.

I followed her gaze and emitted a surprised little gasp of my own. Yes, it was—it most certainly was the illustrious pair. I had to squint through the golden glow surrounding the dancing couples. Over the course of the evening, someone had surreptitiously been dimming the ballroom's overhead lights until they'd been reduced to a flicker, and the tea lights from the tables as well as the after-hours lighting that shone from the base of the exhibits had taken over the majority of the task of illumination. The big room had shrunk into a very intimate dance party—and romance was in the air.

That particular khaki uniform belonged to Owen Hobart, and he had the gorgeous redhead bridesmaid engulfed in his arms. *Finally.* They'd been sitting at their table like a couple of starstruck mummies for hours. Now he had his head dipped down, his nose near the crown of her head as though he was...sniffing her? Inhaling her delicious perfume, of course.

I stuck out my hand, down by my thigh, and Frankie gave it a surreptitious, but celebratory, low-five pat.

"Hallelujah," she muttered. "Otherwise the evening would've been a total bust in the matchmaking department. Speaking of which"—her voice ticked up a notch—"you'd better come up with a good excuse for the absence of our boss in about ten seconds."

Barbara Segreti was winding her way toward us through the half-empty tables. Her hair was piled on top of her head and wound with pink ribbons, adding a good ten inches to her short, round form which was swathed in a swishy silk maxi-dress sporting a delicate cherry-blossom print. The fabric looked hand-painted and very expensive. Barbara had gone to a lot of trouble.

No, *trouble* wasn't the right word, since she owned the only beauty salon in town. *Effort*, perhaps, was more accurate.

She was panting by the time she reached us. "Is Rupert still sick?" she asked, worry creasing her forehead.

Well, there it was, handed to me on a silver platter. "Still not one-hundred percent," I agreed quickly, not bothering to add that, no matter the state of his health, he'd rather embark on a treasure hunt than sit about, roped into exchanging banal pleasantries. Or that he was still blissfully unaware that the woman in front of us had had a crush on him since they were children when they'd played hide-and-seek in his family's lonely old mansion.

Frankie and I were certainly working on Barbara's case—without her explicit consent, I might add—but these things do take time. A *long* time. Barbara had been waiting nearly fifty years.

"Ah, well," she sighed, and shuffled around beside me so she could also watch the dancing couples. "It's been a fine party. No hitches?" She quirked a painted-on brow and a sidelong glance at me.

I shook my head silently. None that I could admit to.

Except what was that sudden cluster over by the hallway to the kitchen? I spotted my husband, standing tall next to a bent-over person, also in a khaki uniform. He waved to me urgently.

Frankie and I scrabbled across the room, shoving chairs out of the way and squeaking between tables. Barbara chose to sail around the perimeter of the room—her small feet must've been churning madly under that tent of a dress—and almost beat us there.

"What's wrong?" I wheezed, already kneeling down beside Sheriff Marge. Pete had managed to prop her into a chair, but she was still bent at the waist and gripping her knees, panting, her face a sickly white.

"Pain," she gasped.

"Where?"

"Right side." Pete set her hat on the table and squatted down beside me. "Came on really fast." The muscles along his jaw were bunched tightly.

"Appendix?"

But Sheriff Marge shook her head. "Had that...taken out...thirty years ago." She was clammy with the strain of breathing, and even her lips were colorless.

"Kidney stone," Barbara announced over our shoulders, with an air of authority.

We were huddled like a football offense, with our disabled quarterback in the center. I tipped my head back to peer at Barbara. "Are you sure?" She was a hairstylist, not a doctor. "Maybe it's indigestion, heartburn, acid reflux."

"I'm right here," Sheriff Marge growled, although her voice was muffled because she was still doubled over and speaking into her knees. "I didn't eat too much. Didn't feel like eating."

"Is it more painful than being in labor?" Barbara insisted.

Sheriff Marge grunted. "Yeah. Been a while since I did that too, but yeah." She was certainly panting with carefully controlled breaths that mimicked the Lamaze technique.

Pete shifted, probably embarrassed at the highly personal direction the conversation was taking. He was the lone male in our huddle, and the urgent topic had just taken on a decidedly intimate flavor.

"Kidney stone," Barbara said with a finality that indicated vast experience. "You need to go to urgent care. You'll need an IV, pain killers, probably a smooth-muscle relaxant."

"Okay."

Sheriff Marge's voice came out like a whisper, but I was so shocked I almost fell over. She was *agreeing* to go to the hospital? This was serious indeed.

Pete jumped up. "I'll get you a driver."

No one was thinking of calling an ambulance. There were three deputies on scene, all of whom were qualified to drive very fast and had sirens and flashing lightbars on the tops of their cars. The closest one happened to be Owen Hobart.

Owen had a blissful sort of dreamy expression on his face, and his eyelids where half closed. But he snapped to reality in an instant when Pete laid a hand on his shoulder for a hasty whispered consultation. And left poor

Darcy bewildered and alone in the middle of the dance floor in his urgency to see to his chief.

"Oh dear," Frankie murmured. "Oh dear." But she rushed to clear a path and open the glass double doors.

We tried to keep the mass exodus quiet, tried not to interrupt the festivities, but when there's a galvanized blitz of khaki, everyone tends to notice.

Sheriff Marge was grumbling the whole way, and waddled forward surrounded by her deputies while still bent in half. "It'll pass," she wheezed, her arms clenched over her abdomen. "Whatever it is, it'll pass."

"Darn tootin'," Barbara affirmed. "It'll pass all right. But you won't like it much." She'd stationed herself at Sheriff Marge's side and was leading her like a small child toward the exit.

This was a side of Barbara I hadn't seen before, but I was grateful for her take-charge attitude, especially when she was going up against the greatest take-charger of them all in Sheriff Marge. And because Sheriff Marge just might need another woman for company in this particular situation when all of her deputies were men. And because I remembered with a startled gasp out in the parking lot that I couldn't be that woman—no matter how much I wanted to be—or be part of the entourage to the hospital.

"I have a kid," I said dazedly to no one in particular, blinking in the frigid air. I felt as though I'd just been splashed in the face with ice water. "I have a kid," I repeated and glanced back at the museum where a few lights burned brightly from an office on the third floor.

"Yeah, babe, we have a kid," Pete said grimly, coming up to wrap an arm around my shoulders.

It was only then that I realized I was shivering uncontrollably, as we watched all the law enforcement personnel rapidly depart—no sirens, but lights swooping across the frozen landscape in a bizarre sort of red and blue ballet, speeding one of their own into Lupine for medical treatment.

~oOo~

The party had come to a screeching halt. That much was clear from the sea of worried and inquisitive faces that were aimed in our direction when we reentered the museum.

Frankie immediately went over to reassure the bereft Darcy. To tell her this sort of thing wasn't normal. Although if she was going to date (as we all hoped—it was a long shot, but hope burns eternal) a deputy, she might as well get used to it.

There was one deputy spouse in attendance—Dale Larson's. He was the only deputy who'd managed to marry and have a mostly normal family life, complete with two kids who were already more than a handful at eight and ten years old. Sandy Larson was a calm and sensible woman, and I liked her immensely.

She had also stationed herself just inside the double doors and caught my elbow. "You'll need to make an announcement," she whispered. "Poor Sheriff Marge, but the rumors..." She shook her head. "There's no confidentiality in Sockeye County."

I knew exactly what she meant. If we didn't tell everyone what was going on, they'd manufacture worse scenarios—like terminal cancer, or leprosy, or brain disease, or something. Sheriff Marge would be dead by morning if left up to the imaginations of the populace.

Pete did the honors. "Sorry, folks," he said, not having to raise his voice at all since every eye was glued on him and the guests seemed to be holding their collective breaths. The band had quit at some point, too—they were stiff as statues up on the temporary dais. "Bit of a scare there, but Sheriff Marge is fully conscious and ambulatory and able to talk. She was complaining about having to leave the party early, actually." Several titters and murmurs of approval ran through the crowd. "She probably just needs to rest a bit—you all know how hard she works—and will be mighty embarrassed if she hears the reception fell into the doldrums after she left. So, Mac and Val," Pete called, lifting an arm to point a challenge at the understandably concerned couple, and his face split into a wide grin. "When are you going to feed these fine people cake?"

Whoops of agreement sounded from the throng, and then the chant of "Kiss, kiss, kiss!" Just like that, the festivities were in full and unabashed swing again.

CHAPTER 17

It was a weird letdown. This being grown-up business. I chafed against the responsibility of staying behind and caring for Burke when I wanted to chase down to the hospital and loiter in the dismal waiting area in order to catch a word—a good word, hopefully—about Sheriff Marge. She'd be okay—Barbara had seemed so matter-of-fact about her condition, but I was accustomed to doing whatever I wanted to, whenever I wanted to.

My very own little charge was sitting at the kitchen table once again, blissfully chowing down his breakfast. And it was good to see him so unconcerned, so childlike. How desperately he needed that. It was a pity he hadn't been able to play with the Larsons' two kids at the reception. They'd have had a blast with hide-and-seek in the mansion's nooks and crannies.

Pete seemed to sense my mood, because he corralled me up against the kitchen sink and started laying on the kisses pretty thick. I might have giggled. That just spurred him on, and his hands began roaming into tickle territory in earnest. Plus, he hadn't shaved yet, and his stubble on my neck made me squirm.

We were interrupted by an eleven-year-old making gagging noises.

I jumped back, worried, rapidly scanning my memory about how to do the Heimlich maneuver.

But Burke was rolling his eyes, and crammed another piece of toast into his mouth. "Gross," he announced around a wad of masticated bread. "I'm gonna lose my appetite if I have to watch *that* every morning."

I blinked at Pete.

His body had stiffened, and an exasperated breath escaped. His voice was calm, but slow and in that lower register that carries a warning, when he said, "You have several options. You can close your eyes. You can leave the room. Or you can watch and learn because loving your lady is an excellent skill to have in your arsenal. But the one option you *don't* have is making sarcastic comments."

Just like that, he'd laid down the law. I was still blinking.

So was Burke, who appeared mildly shocked. And contrite.

Pete's hard gaze was boring into him.

"Okay," he mumbled, ducking his head.

Pete nodded, then wrapped an arm around my waist, pulled me in close, and turned to flick on the kitchen tap. Behind us, a chair was scootched back, and soft footsteps retreated to the stairs.

I tried to angle my head to look over my shoulder, but Pete squeezed me tighter.

"Let him go," he murmured in my ear. "This is a two-way deal. We've chosen him, but for this to work, he has to choose us, too. And he needs to know what he's getting into. That there will be rules, including rules he doesn't like sometimes."

"*Loving your lady is an excellent skill to have in your arsenal?*" I whispered back.

Pete cracked a grin. "Did you like that? Came up with it on the spur of the moment."

"He's eleven," I objected.

"And interested, in spite of his protestations otherwise. Believe me, it happens." Pete's grin spread even wider, then he leaned in to nibble my earlobe. "He might as well learn about proper wooing procedures from the best."

I laughed aloud. I couldn't help it. Maybe parenting wouldn't be so bad after all.

~oOo~

I had to let Jim Carter into the museum so he could cart away all the tables and chairs before we resumed regular visitor hours. Cleaning up ended up being a family affair of the extended variety because Frankie and Henry and Rupert showed up as well. Many hands make light work, or something like that.

The truth was, Rupert and Burke hightailed it into the deep recesses of the third-floor office once again. Which enabled the rest of us to converse normally about the highly debated topics du jour as we passed one another with armloads of decorations and bulging trash bags and mops and brooms and the ancient Hoover with the dangerously frayed cord.

"It means he's feeling comfortable with you," Frankie said during one passing.

"Really?" I croaked. I'd told her about the incident with the fake gagging, and she'd giggled along with me.

"Right," she added on the next pass. "It's like when you bring a puppy home from the pound. It takes a few days for their true personality to emerge, and then they start testing the boundaries. Perfectly normal."

"But he's been through so much trauma," I mused. "How do we even know what's normal for him?"

"He's still a kid. And he'll behave in kid fashion. He'll go through phases. And have hormones. You'll see."

I decided to take her word for it. I needed all the good advice I could get.

In mid-afternoon, Owen Hobart stopped by. "Figured I'd find you here," he said after pushing through the double glass doors and scrunching his nose at the stench of Pine-Sol. He looked exhausted and was still in the same khaki uniform from the night before. I was fifty-percent sure, at any rate, khaki uniforms all looking pretty much the same.

"How is she?" I asked, pausing in the wide arc I was making with a sudsy mop. The wedding cake frosting had turned into thin smears of sugary concrete wherever it had come into contact with the parquet oak floor.

"Grouchy," Owen sighed, and rubbed his left eye.

"That's a given." Frankie tiptoed around the wet spots and joined us. "Diagnosis? Prognosis?"

"Well, she's pretty groggy from the painkillers, and they're having her uh, well, uh..."

"Strain her urine?" Frankie spared him the embarrassment of saying it out loud by doing it herself. To my great delight, I'd been finding that middle-aged (and older) women tend to be fans of stating it like it is. Beating around the bush is a waste of words and time.

Owen nodded. "Several of my buddies over in Iraq had recurring kidney stones. The desert conditions over there make it harder to avoid. Hurts like hell, or so I've been told. Good reason to never get dehydrated."

"Amen," Frankie said.

"But how *is* she?" I insisted.

"Out of commission until the doctor clears her, until she passes the stone. Normally a kidney stone is an outpatient kind of problem, but they're not taking any chances with Sheriff Marge, much to her intense irritation. Which means"—Owen reached into his chest pocket and pulled out a small notebook in a maneuver that almost exactly replicated his boss's technique—"I have some more questions to ask, on her behalf."

"First things first." Frankie held out her feather duster like a magic wand. "What about your skills as an investigator?"

Owen frowned, shifted his weight. "I've been taking classes," he said, trying hard, I thought, not to sound defensive. "I'm about fifteen hours away from meeting the detective training qualifications. Then I need to take the test."

"And yet," Frankie said sternly, "you forgot to ask a young lady for her phone number."

Owen blushed furiously. "It was an emergency. I had to go..."

"Never mind." Frankie patted his arm. "I covered your behind and made your apologies." She fished in her jeans pocket and handed him a crumpled piece of paper. "You can thank me later."

Owen took a quick peek at the writing on the scrap and shifted some more, most adorably. His flush had turned the color of the volunteer fire department's engine. "She's uh...it would be okay?" he croaked.

"Oh, I'd say better than okay." Frankie beamed, but then she stuck out a forefinger and tapped his chest. "But no tarrying, young man. You need to make that call by tomorrow at the latest, investigation or no investigation." In a rare display of role-reversal, she was letting him go with a stiff warning. I'm not sure I successfully hid my grin.

"Yes, ma'am," Owen answered meekly and carefully pocketed the precious paper.

"So, these questions." I cleared my throat, getting down to business. "Are we going to need coffee?"

Owen rubbed his right eye. "That'd be good."

The poor fellow. He was obviously running on fumes.

"Coming right up," Frankie said over her shoulder as she bustled toward the kitchen. "I'll call the guys, too. I'm assuming you'll need all brains on deck."

It was a familiar scene, this confab around the lunch table in the Imogene's kitchen, all of us perched on the cold, uncompromising seats of metal folding chairs. Many secrets had been spilled, heartbreaks shared, and puzzles solved in this very place over my short tenure at the museum. Maybe it was an emotional vortex. I wasn't sure about the magneto-electric vibes, but I was definitely glad to have Pete's long, strong thigh to rest my own against, and the warmth of his shoulder next to me.

Pete and Henry had been at the cabin when Cassidy's body had been found. If anyone had insight for Sheriff Marge's questions, it'd be them. Frankie and I were there just for moral support—and for the coffee. It'd been a long, rigorous day, and my muscles were starting to ache.

There was nothing wrong with Owen's tongue now. He assumed leadership of the session with confidence and a keen attention to detail. He was organizing the disparate facts the same way I outline my research into historical items for display in the museum, trying to flesh out the skeleton of basic information into a compelling story. It was familiar—and therefore somewhat comforting— territory. Even though my analogy gave me the shudders, considering the very real *skeleton* he was investigating.

"First off," he said, wincing after he'd downed half a cup of scalding coffee, "I need to know what the buzz was about at the reception."

None of us pointed out the fact that Owen *had* been present at the reception. He'd just been thoroughly and delightfully distracted. Which we didn't point out either. And, from my own experience, I knew that different people heard different things, so this would be an interesting experiment.

Henry glanced around at all of us, then said in response to our nods, "I'll go first. I did hear a few murmurs about the murder, but those same speakers seemed to quickly divert into tales of other illegal activities up on Gifford Mountain. It's a place of lore, apparently, and nobody seems too startled by any report of devious behavior up there. They seem to be taking it in stride." He paused to sip from his Styrofoam cup and then sniffed. "The much more prevalent conversation was about the crops. I'd heard it from some of my neighbors even before the reception—that the winter wheat is coming in strong, with a very high germination rate."

"But..." Pete interrupted.

"Yeah, *but*," Henry agreed, nodding. "They're also upset about not getting their rebates." He spent the next few minutes reiterating what Pete had already explained to me, about the unfair nature of SeedGenix's promises and their questionable validation methods—or rather the promises made by their sales reps. No one was sure if the company would honor the verbal agreements of what were perhaps rogue salesmen. Then again, the fact that so many different reps had offered rebates seemed to indicate they'd been prompted to do so by the higher-ups in the organization. It was a matter of much debate and speculation.

Then it was Frankie's turn. She was making fingernail indentations in the rim of her Styrofoam cup and biting her lips. "I, uh, I may have heard some of that," she admitted. "But..." She flashed a concerned glance across the table at me.

I cringed in sympathy. I knew what she'd been up to during the party, but saying so out loud, in mixed company, was another matter. "Administrative duties," I offered.

She jumped at the explanation. "Yes!" And accidentally decapitated her cup, having indented the rim to the point of structural failure. A few dribbles of coffee puddled on the table.

I leaped up to snatch a paper towel off the roll. The problem was, matchmaking in Sockeye County was women's work. We didn't discuss our strategic initiatives with the men. Poor guys probably wouldn't appreciate all the effort and finagling that went into happily-ever-afters. Too easy to interpret all our carefully laid plans as manipulation.

"So, I was, uh, introducing people," she finally said as she accepted the paper towel from me and mopped up her spill. "Making sure everyone was getting along, you know, and meeting new friends."

Owen's eyes had narrowed suspiciously. "Were you in charge of the seating assignments?"

"I helped," I blurted before Frankie could answer. "And so did Rupert." Easier to blame the museum director when he was still embedded in his office upstairs. Also, because it was true, especially regarding the random selection of a certain Darcy O'Hare to fill a slot at Owen's table.

Group guilt—that way Owen couldn't blame one single person for his future happiness. Hopefully.

"So I was mixing a lot—mingling—and only sticking with any small group of people long enough to make sure they were happy, well fed, and knew where the bathrooms are," Frankie finished. "Hostess stuff, you know."

Prudent man that he is, Owen didn't pursue her statement further. Instead, he fixed his interrogator's gaze on me.

Truthfully, I didn't have much to add, except the petty theft and vandalism angle.

Owen snorted softly. "Sheriff Marge told me to ask you how the exhibit is coming along. Even hyped up on Vicodin, she's dead set on nipping this blight in the bud."

I groaned inwardly. "Working on it as fast as I can. It's just—" I flapped a hand ineffectually—"there's a lot going on."

Owen shared a wry grin with me. "I don't suppose you've found the case from the 1930s where a deputy charged twenty-five cents per person for admission to a grisly murder scene that he was supposed to be guarding? That's one of my favorites. Before DNA testing existed, but still. Souvenirs were taken, the place was trampled. Needless to say, we no longer allow the general public anywhere near our crime scenes," he added, "at least not knowingly." And with that he tipped glances at Pete and Henry who gave him grim nods in return.

Once again, I wondered just exactly what they'd seen. My mind was intensely curious, my stomach not so much. I swallowed. But Owen's comments about the developing exhibit rejuvenated my motivation even more, and the idea of a life-size crime scene diorama popped into my head. Who wouldn't want to walk through a reproduced site from the past and try to solve the crime themselves? Like an in situ game of Clue. I clasped my hands together under the table and started mentally pacing off the open space in the empty half of the former sitting room in the northwest corner of the Imogene's second floor. It was dark back there, not too many windows, which would make it perfect for a highly atmospheric exhibit.

"Meredith?" Owen said.

I snapped out of my reverie and realized everyone was staring at me. "Uh, nothing. I mean, that's it. I have nothing else to add," I babbled.

Pete rubbed my shoulder. Ugh. He, unfortunately, has some knowledge of how my mind works. But he filled in my gap and began his own recitation of his observations from the reception. He kept it short—it was old news by now.

Having exhausted our civilian gossiping prowess, Owen heaved a sigh and rubbed both of his eyes. "Well, that fits."

CHAPTER 18

Was that a tiny admission that Deputy Owen Hobart knew more than he was letting on? We all sat up straighter on our chairs. Of course he did. After such a thorough collective grilling, a bit of tit for tat was in order.

"Spill it, young man," Frankie said in her no-nonsense voice.

Owen shook his head. "Where to start? It's not good."

So I decided to refill his cup with lukewarm coffee. It was the least I could do. Outside, snow was falling thickly, almost like the smothering foam from a firefighting aircraft. I could barely see blotchy patches of the trees in the park through the fat, fluffy flakes.

I stayed by the window after resupplying Owen. My calves were starting to cramp from the day of manual labor and they needed stretching. Besides, who doesn't want to look at a world of soft and downy purity while hearing the latest details about a grisly murder? The contrast was almost unfathomable.

"Sheriff McNary over in Whitman County is giving us all the help he can," Owen began. "The loss of Cassidy has hit their small community hard. She was their golden girl. Through him we have a lead on the pickup. One matching the description—the really comprehensive description—that Burke gave us was reported stolen from the parking lot next to the administration building on the Washington State University campus."

"That place is huge," Pete said.

"Exactly. And fairly anonymous with as many students as they have. It's like stealing a vehicle from an international airport's long-term parking lot. Same sort of acreage, and most pedestrians, if any, not giving a second thought to someone climbing into a pickup."

"Are you saying there are no leads, then?" Henry asked.

"Right. It's sketchy. We're ninety percent sure that's the vehicle that was used, but we don't know who took it or where it is now. If we could find it now, we might be able to get some evidence—DNA, rope fibers, maybe even muddy footprints from the floor mats, but until then..."

"No cameras?" Pete asked.

Owen shook his head. "Not in their budget yet. The higher crime areas around the dormitories are covered because drunk students do stupid stuff, but they haven't had much problem in the admin parking lot, so coverage there was back-burnered until more funds can be earmarked."

"And the owner of the pickup?" Frankie asked.

I smiled grimly as I tipped my forehead against the cold glass of the window. My batch of loved ones was doing a good job of holding our own in the interrogation department.

"Not a suspect. He was at work all day; came out to find his truck gone. Got a ride home from a coworker, filed a stolen vehicle report immediately, and is a research coordinator of good standing with the university. Sheriff McNary knows him personally and says he's meeker than a church mouse. No vitriol in that guy."

"And you believe him?" Frankie pushed.

Owen nodded. "We have to. It's his turf."

"But a research coordinator," I murmured to the window and the incongruously peaceful setting beyond. That wasn't quite true—the setting inside was also peaceful enough, a bunch of friends sharing coffee while seated on uncomfortable chairs. It was the content that was disturbing.

My words must've bounced off the glass, because Owen answered as though he'd heard them clearly. "Yeah, this is where it starts to get interesting. I called Cassidy's dissertation adviser, and we had a lengthy chat about her research. She was big on wheat, meticulous in her attention to detail. He couldn't say enough good things about her. She was pioneering the use of a special meter affixed to a drone for measuring the molecular composition of the air at various elevations above the crop. Apparently the rate at which the plants expire oxygen and uptake carbon dioxide indicates the quality of their photosynthesis, and all that can be measured in order to evaluate the density and health of the crop." Owen plunked his elbows on the table. "A little over my head, frankly."

"Do doctoral students get grants for their research?" I asked. "This sounds expensive. Who was footing the bill? Surely not Cassidy. The university?" I know how hard it is to get a grant, having applied for several and having received an almost equal number of rejections.

Owen shifted in his seat to fix me with a steady gaze. "SeedGenix."

Pete blew out a breath and slumped back in his chair. "Oh boy."

"Wait," said Henry. "Does that make everyone who complained about the nonexistent rebates at the party last night a suspect? Is that why you were asking?"

"Indirectly, yeah, until we narrow it down," Owen admitted. "But practically, no—it's a really long shot. Meredith's right, though. We have to continue following the money."

"So, are you saying," I spouted, desperately needing clarification, "that Cassidy was our up-and-coming third-party verification source for germination rate, but that in reality she also was being paid by SeedGenix?"

"Yes." Owen stretched out an arm and squeezed the back of his neck while shaking his head slowly from side to side. He looked like he ached all over too—and needed about thirty hours of sleep. "Complicated. But I'm given to understand that these very close ties and intertwined payment structures are normal between companies and research universities. What's good for one tends to be good for the other."

"Until it isn't," Pete muttered. He was standing now too, and began pacing back and forth on the black and white tiles.

But Henry, the retired army helicopter mechanic and experimental pilot in his own right, was still worried about a practical matter. "Was the drone equipped with a camera as well as the air-content meter thing?"

Owen nodded.

"So the real question might be," Henry continued, almost under his breath, "what did she *see* with that drone? I assume there was footage, a recording?"

"Gone." Owen got to his feet as well, and leaned on the back of his chair, his hands gripping the rim so hard his knuckles were white. "Cassidy's equipment disappeared along with her, and hasn't resurfaced, unlike her, uh...her body. But if she did see something, or record something sensitive, I don't think she realized it. Because she never reported anything untoward to her adviser, and Burke's description of her behavior on the day of her murder was that she was happy, cheerful, even eager, up until the very instant the noose was slipped over her head."

We had a moment—a fraction of a moment, really—of warning. Enough time to not fill the sickly silence that had followed Owen's words, but not enough time to readjust our expressions into something less horrified, less appalled, less confused.

So when Rupert and a small boy trotted headlong into the room, we were rooted in position like queasy statues. Rupert took one look at our collective trepidation and immediately began to backpedal, causing Burke to bump into him, hard.

"Ooof," Rupert grunted, bracing himself against the door frame and squinting apologetically at us. "Sorry, so sorry. We figured you'd be in here, needing a break and whatnot, from all the cleanup. And we have...well, we've found what we were looking for."

Burke was in Rupert's lee, a small and immediately hesitant shadow. The delighted and enthusiastic expression on his little face had faded to hollow concern in a transition so fast it nearly broke my heart. Once again, those huge eyes missed nothing.

So I tried to smile at him. "Let's see." I held out my hand.

He shuffled into the kitchen and thrust a jumbled assortment of three-dimensional items at me. We fumbled them for a moment in the space between us, and I giggled.

Burke's big eyes flashed up to me in hopefulness, and I realized that he assumed we'd been talking about him—which had definitely been the case. But underlying that, there was a worry, an uncertainty, that maybe somehow he'd disappointed us.

I had to squat down to hold all the items securely, and that also gave me a chance to wrap an arm around his thin back and pull him closer. "Tell me what these are," I murmured.

"Badges," he complied, pointing. "Rupert says these were for hats." He picked up two of the badges and turned them over, revealing both the screw mounts and the engraved numbers matched to each of the long-gone Pinkerton detectives on the backs. His soft voice was tinged with a little bit of awe and a lot of eagerness. "And here's a flat shield badge that would've been pinned on the agent's chest. It's from the Canada department—see the maple leaves?" His handling of the treasured bit of history was both confident and delicate.

The final item was a very small, pearl-grip revolver. It was old and nicked but had originally been rather showy. I thought it might've been a stage prop until Burke showed me the inscription. A presentation handgun to a lieutenant in the Pennsylvania state militia for helping quell the Homestead Riots in 1892. In a case where the National Guard had been called in because the Pinkerton agents had failed. From the reverential way Burke was holding the gun, I guessed that Rupert had told him the history. Men on both sides of the labor dispute had died unnecessarily.

I suffered a sudden, gut-wrenching wave of grief for the child before me—again. Would it never stop? For him or for me?

"Do you like it?" I whispered.

He nodded, those eyes magnificent in the fading silver light from the snowstorm outside.

"We'll find the perfect way to display it, and you can help me write the description that we'll post next to it, okay?"

More nodding.

"Show me that it's empty?"

And he did, expertly to my uninitiated way of viewing, clicking the barrel to the side and revealing the empty chambers where the bullets would've fit. The kid knew too much—far, far too much.

Every test I put in front of him, he passed, with flying colors. I would've preferred a little more normalcy, a little more uncertainty, a little more averageness on the bell curve, a little more childishness.

Except for the gagging this morning. That little scenario was looking more and more like comic relief in the grand scale of his overall situation.

We had a rapt audience. This dawned on me abruptly, and I stood. "Thank you," I said to Rupert. "They're perfect."

He nodded knowingly. "I thought they'd fit the theme."

The powwow was over. Owen drained the last of the cold coffee in his cup and left the room without speaking.

Frankie collected the dirty cups and swiped a sponge over the tabletop. "Just a few more things to tidy, then we're out of here. Are you going to do a walk-through?" she added in a lower tone as she brushed by me.

After I nodded—she knew me well—she said more brightly, "Then perhaps Pete and Burke would like a ride with us? We'll drop you two at the farmhouse, and Meredith can catch up later."

Pete gave me a smile and a squeeze—he knew me well, too—and they all trooped out.

Peace. Quiet. I needed both. My deep well of solitude was clamoring for replenishment. Being married doesn't obliterate introversion. Temporary and unexpected motherhood even less so.

And I love this old museum. She's my girl. And she needed an inspection to make sure she was ready for visitors. The last thing we wanted was for a tourist to find a leftover plate with the ant-eaten remains of a piece of wedding cake wedged behind the stuffed and mounted cougar in the library or someone's forgotten—and very modern—gloves dropped in the middle of the Victorian ball gown display. Besides, there was the sitting room to measure off for the new exhibit.

~oOo~

All was as it should be, much to my relief and satisfaction. The Imogene was in her usual, if slightly derelict, state and clean as a whistle. We try our best to spruce her up, but she's expensive to maintain. Ideas for the sitting room display sequence were now percolating in my mind. It was good to have something to focus on.

I worked backward through the museum, locking the front doors and checking the windows. Most are painted shut, but you never know if some slightly inebriated and flushed wedding guest might've tried to jimmy one open anyway, and with a peculiar persistence due to the celebratory proceedings.

In the kitchen I tied up the trash bag from under the sink and flipped it over my shoulder like a hobo. Then it was down the stairs to the basement for a quick perusal. The public weren't allowed below, so I wasn't expecting anything to be amiss, but I feel better when I've checked every corner.

Miss Racy Fishnet Stockings was still decently covered, and I grinned at her shroud. History really is a matter of curation, unfortunately. How much have we lost over the years due to cultural gatekeepers putting the kibosh on unpleasant or embarrassing facts? Our human experience has been highly edited for content. And I play a part in that. For good, or for bad? Sometimes I wonder.

And I was getting maudlin in my isolation. So it was time to go.

I poked the alarm key code for all zones into the touchpad, bumped open the basement door with my hip, flipped the lever to lock it, and let it swing closed behind me and my burden. I scuffed up the ramp in heavy, wet snow that came up to the middle of my shins.

We don't usually have so much accumulation, the Columbia River Gorge preferring her winter precipitation in the form of rain and, on rough days, ice. Snow was a treat—until it wasn't. But the kids would enjoy being absolved from school. Which reminded me that at some point we'd need to enroll Burke. Perhaps Hester Maxwell, the social worker, would have suggestions about easing him into that standard practice of childhood—one of many he'd missed out on. For good, or for bad?—I couldn't draw a firm conclusion on that topic, either. He already knew too much.

A gray Acura sedan was parked next to the dumpster, wedged backward into the very narrow space on the north end. I flung the trash bag with my very best discus-throw technique over the top rim of the dumpster and went to check on the vehicle. It had a skim of snow on the windshield, and I brushed open a peephole.

Empty.

That was the most important thing. As long as there wasn't someone inside, shivering while waiting for a tow truck. It's not uncommon for vehicles to be left for a day or two in the main parking lot, just a consequence of the lot's proximity to State Route 14, really. It's a convenient and out-of-the-way place to seek shelter if someone's having mechanical difficulties.

But around back behind the museum is a different matter. However, given the number of guests we'd had at the wedding reception, I was certain some of them would've had to avail themselves of the more remote spaces to park. To still be here, though, was concerning.

Nothing seemed obviously amiss with the vehicle, and the tire tracks where it had backed into the spot were almost refilled to level with the falling snow. Footprints—if there had been any—were long gone. Washington plates.

I breathed a quiet sigh of relief that the museum's new alarm system was finally installed and fully—and reliably—operational. We hadn't had any of those buggy false-alarm triggers with this new system. The old one had been so hair-trigger prone to overassumptions that Rupert had insisted we stop using it so we didn't drive Sheriff Marge and her deputies crazy. Which had left our artifacts at risk, especially the Bronze Age collection tucked away in the laundry room in the basement that no one was supposed to know about until the FBI secured its safe return to its Middle Eastern country of origin. Since that process would likely require decades of negotiations, our insurance company had helped foot the bill for the necessary new, robust, and hopefully infallible alarm system. The Imogene was like Fort Knox now.

So I contentedly tromped through snow drifts in the landscaping around the mansion to the main parking lot where my pickup waited, cold and a little balky on the starter. But on the third try her engine roared to life with that strong and steady thump that makes everything— including me on the bench seat—rattle. I love being surrounded by the old, the faithful, and the familiar.

But don't tell Pete that. He might not take it as a compliment.

CHAPTER 19

The *Surely* was docked in port for scheduled maintenance. Winter's a slow time for Pete, and he loves to make sure her two big marine diesel engines purr like...I don't know...not a kitten, because that would just be ridiculous. Maybe like the biggest, hungriest saber-toothed tiger you've never seen. The *Surely* is small for her class, but she's mighty, and she can maneuver loads into and out of the tightest spots, making her much in demand during the other three seasons. This is due entirely to the skill of her master. Not that I'm biased or anything.

But she gets pampered in the winter to make up for her hard work during the rest of the year, and Pete offered to take Burke along for a little grease-monkey action since they'd be stationary for the day, and I was glad of the break. Besides, what boy doesn't need to know how to replenish the oil in a V12 7200 horsepower motor? The noise of those babies running—singly, let alone in tandem—is enough to knock you off your feet.

So I spent the morning humming quietly to myself while scritching masking tape across the floor in the Imogene's former sitting room. The new exhibit, complete with interactive displays, although still in its developmental stage, was coming along nicely.

Frankie nearly scared the hooey out of me when she came up behind me in her soft-soled therapeutic loafers.

"What are you doing here?" I gasped, clutching at my chest. The museum is closed on Mondays, and the staff—all two of us—are *supposed* to take the day off.

"Same thing you are, I reckon."

I squinted at her. "Which is?"

"Keeping busy so you don't fret as much. Is it working?"

"No." I slid the three empty masking tape rolls I'd been wearing as bracelets off my forearm and let them clatter to the floor. The way things were going, I'd need to run to the store to pick up more supplies. "I wish police work—detecting—wasn't so tedious. So *slow*."

"It's been, what, four days since Cassidy's body was found? Just a week since Burke appeared in your—our—lives?" As always, Frankie was the voice of reason. I suspected it had to do with her helmet hair—perhaps that layer of shellac forced her brain into pragmatic thoughts.

"Something like that," I mumbled. So I decided to turn the tables on her. "You *did* make a copy of Darcy's phone number, didn't you? Just in case our swamped-with-work deputy forgets?"

Frankie smacked her rear jeans pocket with a wink. "Available at a moment's notice."

"You're incorrigible." I couldn't help grinning at her.

"Right back at you, honey." Frankie waggled a finger at the maze I'd created on the floor with the masking tape. "Make a list of what you need. I'll do your shopping for you."

Was I really that obvious? Clearly, the answer was yes. I squeezed her shoulders in appreciation and resumed measuring and diagramming.

Until the rapid thudding of rubber sneakers on the parquet oak floor interrupted me—Burke, face shining underneath a smattering of grease smears, who was followed more sedately by my incredibly hunky husband. I will never get tired of looking at that man, no matter how smudged and worn his jeans are or how much black grime is embedded under his fingernails. He works hard, and I love him for it—among other reasons.

"That was fast," I said, straightening and wincing while the cricks in my back readjusted themselves. I, also, would never complain about not having a desk job—never in a million years—and not even when my morning consists of waddling while bent in half with my fingertips within sticking distance of the floor. It's not graceful, but it gets the job done.

"We covered the basics," Pete said, "but I got a call from Delbert Mason, out in Arlington. He wants me to consult on a project he's thinking about."

I frowned. This isn't unusual—farmers soliciting Pete's help in solving logistical problems. It goes with the territory. But usually the requests are last-minute, when the technique they'd been trying fails miserably, borderline catastrophically, and they call Pete more for a rescue than for an assist.

Pete read my mind. "Not sure why he called me now, but it's quiet. I can spare a trip out there to see what he's thinking about. Dredging, most likely. He might want to open up a bigger staging area to accommodate more barges during harvest. The Coast Guard will have to approve it, and their permit applications can be tricky." Pete shrugged. "Might just be paperwork."

And therefore boring. Which explained the hand-off of our small charge, who'd busied himself with walking, heel-to-toe, along my masking tape lines, arms outstretched for balance. Also, there was no good reason for a co-op manager out in Arlington to know that Pete now had a tagalong boy. That would prompt a lot of questions we weren't at liberty to answer just now.

Pete and I weren't saying a lot, but the thoughts were zinging back and forth. He was watching me closely with those crinkle-cornered sapphire-blue eyes and a faint grin on his face, then he moved in to give me a good-bye kiss.

There were no gakky noises from the peanut gallery this time.

"I'll be late," Pete whispered, his arms strong and warm around me. "You'll be okay?"

"No. I'll be pining away for you," I whispered back, and gave him an extra kiss in the soft spot under his ear for good measure.

~oOo~

Burke should get paid intern wages. Sadly, the Imogene Museum isn't in the habit of remunerating interns, counting instead on their general goodwill and volunteer generosity, our budget being somewhat restricted. And more importantly, perhaps, the board of directors would have severe ethical difficulties with employing child labor.

But he was a cheerful helper, and we made significant progress in plotting out the paths of the life-size forensic diorama during the next hour. He also had been thinking deeply about his potential living situation, judging by the nature of the slew of questions he lobbed at me.

He started with, "Why don't you and Pete have kids?"

"We just got married a few months ago. Haven't had time to think about it, really." I shrugged and double-checked a measurement with my laser sight. The exhibit needed to be wheelchair accessible, and that necessitated sufficient width in the aisles of the diorama.

"Are you going to have kids?" he persisted. Good grief. The nosy matrons of Sockeye County had nothing on the boy.

"I don't know. There are a lot of variables in that equation. We're still working on, you know, getting along with each other, first and foremost."

Burke snorted derisively. "You get along fine. All that smooching." He rolled his eyes, but I wasn't going to validate his reaction by letting him know I'd seen the snarky motion.

"I'm pretty sure your parents smooched a time or two as well." As soon as the words were out of my mouth, I regretted them. He didn't need a reminder of what he'd lost.

Burke responded immediately with a heavy sigh. "Yeah." He stomped on a skittering dust bunny the size of a great-granddaddy cockroach that had been released from a corner with all of our bustling.

With his head bent and his shaggy hair hanging in his eyes, I couldn't read his expression. How *do* kids grieve? Burke had been remarkably mellow about it so far, but he'd also had five months to become accustomed to the idea. The shock was in learning that his father's absence was now permanent rather than temporary. It would undoubtedly take that reality quite some time to sink in.

He flopped his arms awkwardly and balanced on one leg to brush the sole of the dust-bunny-obliterating sneaker on the jeans on his opposite shin. "It's just that I'd kind of like a brother," he continued in a voice so quiet I had to stop writing dimensions in my notebook in order to be able to hear him. His little face scrunched for a reluctant concession, "Or a sister."

It was my turn for a heartfelt exhale. "I can't make that kind of promise. But I understand. I was an only child too. That's probably why I like books so much, not having playmates when I was growing up."

"I wouldn't be bossy," Burke continued, as though he hadn't heard me. "I'd show 'em stuff, and I'd let 'em use my things sometimes. We could even share a room if we had to." Apparently he had it all planned out.

"You'd make a good big brother," I said softly.

"Yeah," he agreed, without a trace of pride.

I took my human-connection starved boy home for an early supper when I could hear his stomach rumbling from across the room.

~oOo~

Cleaning. Cleaning like a madwoman.

I'd spent all day making a mess (new exhibits always look like a disaster zone until they don't—it's a fine line in development), then spent the next hour at home in a flurried frenzy of dusting, vacuuming, and mopping. Tuppence was banished to the back porch until I could remove her footprints and nose smudges from the lower regions of the kitchen.

Because I'd recalled—somewhat belatedly—that our interview with the social worker was on the books for that evening. If I was going to prove that I could care for a child, I also had to prove that I could care for a rambling farmhouse. And I wanted to do so much more than just meet the most basic requirements. I wanted to shine— maybe to demonstrate to myself as well as to Hester Maxwell that I could do this thing called parenting.

It's just that the Tinsleys' gift to us was so much bigger than my fifth-wheel trailer, and I was still learning exactly how much time I needed to allocate to general upkeep, not to mention preventive maintenance. We loved the space, of course, but it required a commensurate commitment in time and elbow grease.

It was also a weird sort of déjà vu of our marathon session at the museum the day before. At least I'd gotten some good practice in.

I'd just spotted a full, dark, Pete-size handprint on the wall below the light switch next to the front door, and had a bottle of Windex poised, trigger primed to obliterate the grease, when a thud on the front porch stopped me cold.

Tuppence hadn't barked. The drapes were closed, so I hadn't seen a sweep of headlights cross the front windows as a car approached. We still had half an hour until the agreed-upon meeting time. And the noise had come from the *front* porch.

I didn't know Hester—yet—but from our brief chat on the phone, she'd struck me as friendly, easy-going, and efficient. The kind of person who'd know to come to the back door, just as Olivia Oliphant had known, and thereby conforming to the standard social practice in these parts.

Noises on the front porch are highly suspect, regardless of the circumstances. Unless it was a wayward raccoon looking for a handout. I tapped the hinged flap on the old-fashioned fish-eye peephole in the front door out of the way and bent to peek through.

That was no Hester Maxwell. He stood like a man. Wiry, slender, stiff with irritation. And behind him was a bigger guy. They were in quiet consultation, pitched toward each other, and standing well to the side of the beam from the front porch light.

The light was on a timer. Out of habit, and for the sake of appearances, even though all coming and going occurred through the back, so it previously hadn't been an issue that it didn't provide the best illumination.

But I'd still seen enough to do some mental matching with Ms. Oliphant's sketches.

The men were casting murky shadows and hunched next to the porch swing. But the height and size discrepancy between the two was another confirming factor. Their relative demeanors were exactly as Burke had described them.

Murderers, standing on my front porch. I forgot how to breathe.

They hadn't actually knocked. The thud I'd heard must've been accidental, and the conversation was so hushed that I couldn't pick up any snatches of it even though I'd tipped my ear toward the crack between the door and the door frame.

"Who is it?" Burke hissed.

He'd been washing the dishes from supper—I'd figured that if he was going to eat so much he might as well learn how to deal with the aftermath—but I'd been concentrating so hard on the distorted view through the peephole that I hadn't heard him as he'd approached. Or maybe he was naturally stealthy as a result of living in hiding in the forest for a couple years. But now he was pressing his body against my hip as though in desperate need for reassuring contact, worry etched across his face. He was too short to see through the peephole himself.

I didn't have enough saliva in my mouth to tell him.

My silence was sufficient—or he read the fear in my eyes—because he grabbed my hand and nearly yanked my shoulder out of its socket.

CHAPTER 20

I wanted walls around me. Solid two-by-four studs bolstered with lath and plaster and paint. Maybe the basement—that glorious concrete box of a bunker deep below ground with shelves stuffed full of Harriet's canning jars.

On second thought, the basement had only one way in—and one way out. Walls were still sounding good, though. Crucial, in fact.

But Burke was insistent as he tugged me toward the back door. "Outside!" he whispered.

"We can hide in here." I planted my feet, but the kitchen linoleum was slick in its newfound cleanliness, and Burke was determined, and I skidded along on the flat soles of my moccasin boots.

"No we can't," he argued breathlessly. "Like fish in a barrel. We have to get out." He continued towing me across the room. "Hurry!"

I had the presence of mind to snatch our coats off the hooks as he barged—somehow silently, unless adrenaline had temporarily turned me deaf—onto the back porch. The kid was a wonder, and I began to wonder myself just how much he knew about hiding and slinking through the woods. Much more than I did, clearly. So far, his instincts had preserved him, and it was perhaps prudent for me to trust them—for both our sakes.

Tuppence scrabbled up from the old blanket she'd been snoozing on, instantly eager, her tail whipping furiously in anticipation of something—anything— exciting. She's always ready to go for a hike.

And trek we did, with our arms pumping and our legs churning—a mad dash in surreally sloggy snow, leaving our gashed footprints behind like find-us-this-way arrows, disturbed only by the prancing circles my dog made around them.

The thing I'd forgotten to grab? My phone.

Already I was missing its comfortable weight in my pocket, but there was no going back now. I risked a hasty glance over my shoulder. No dark, man-shaped silhouettes against the snowy landscape near the house, but that didn't mean there wouldn't be, and soon.

Burke headed straight for the pole barn. I was thinking this strategy was far too obvious, but I was also panting too hard to voice an objection. It was all I could do to keep up with him.

He crashed open the door into the barn—unlocked as well, per usual—and immediately careened around my pickup toward Pete's workbench on the far side.

In weather like this, I park the truck in the pole barn instead of up closer to the house. It saves having to crack ice off the door handles or sweep snow off the windshield the next morning. But the old workhorse did us no good at the moment because my keys, too, were in the house. I don't know how to hot-wire a vehicle's ignition. It's one of those important skills they don't teach you in school. And I suspected that in spite of all his forest-smarts, this was one street-smart Burke didn't have either, not that he could've reached the pedals anyway.

He was making a desperate racket now, flinging scrap lumber and dowels and a spare broom handle and plywood remnants out of Pete's previously neatly organized stash. *Homeowner spares*, Pete liked to call the remaining bits and bobs that were too big and/or too valuable to throw away once a project was finished, always with a note of satisfaction in his tone.

"Here!" Burke called, dragging out a huge, flattened cardboard box. The one our new washing machine had been packaged in. The one that might come in handy if we ever wanted to spray-paint something, according to Pete. This hoarding of potentially useful stuff had been a new aspect of his personality I hadn't known about earlier—probably because neither of us had had the space to store anything beyond the most bare of necessities before. And it was a trait that was taking me some time to get accustomed to.

"Come on!" Burke was flapping his arm, snapping me back to reality, and urging me toward the door on the other side of the barn.

I pushed off from the pickup's fender and dashed across to him, my breathing rate still not having descended into a comfortable zone. Oh, for young legs again, but this was no time for lollygagging.

Burke's intention and ingeniousness became apparent the moment I stepped out into the snow again.

Our property has a gentle slope to it, down to the river. *Gentle* is a relative term, compared to the steep, nearly perpendicular basalt rifts that comprise the majority of towering rock faces through which the Columbia River Gorge has been carved over millennia.

He was already sitting on the flattened cardboard, and I dropped onto the platform behind him and scooted in against him, wrapping my arms around his middle and straddling my legs out alongside his shorter ones.

Burke began rocking furiously, and I reached back and shoved hard against the gravel under the snow, and we were off, tilting backward against the gathering speed and hanging on for dear life.

Our hill has stupendous giddyap-and-go. Within moments, I was breathless again, for a completely different reason. I had to let go of Burke and snatch at the raised cardboard flaps on either side of us, adding my own strength to his for fear that our makeshift transportation would break apart and disintegrate in midair.

Because we did depart terra firma a few times, briefly, and then slammed back down. Snow is not so soft and cushiony as I'd assumed it was. We were two thin layers of paper pulp and some snarled packing tape away from disaster.

There was a rough shout somewhere in the distance behind us. I couldn't look back, but the noise— not stealthy in the slightest—could only mean one thing. We'd been spotted.

But another, madder rush of clamor filled my ears and wiped every other thought except the vital grip of cardboard in my frozen hands from the forefront of my mind. We were screaming through the air now, across that horizonal intersection of gas and solid, the frosty surface whizzing and scraping and juddering below us, sounding like an endless zipper as we hurtled downhill at a pace that was beyond reckless.

My eyelids were stuck open, the lashes iced together, creating a picture frame for our impending doom.

At least we weren't going to sail straight into the frigid water. We were going to splatter all over the side of the intervening railroad berm—the one built from boulders and covered over in the past several decades with a scant layer of wind-deposited soil and a few hardy weeds and now about eight inches of thoroughly misleading snow.

I had a sudden urge to scream—not that it would do any good.

In a rapid reversal of g-forces, we rocketed through the little dip ahead of the berm, pressed like lumps of sodden clay into our cardboard toboggan, then swooped up the side of the berm with a stomach-churning lurch.

Way, way up.

And up.

And up.

Until gravity took over and we rolled back down, heels over heads in a jumble of limbs and joints and boots and flapping coats, and at least one tooth that went through my lower lip.

CHAPTER 21

"Are you dead?" The small voice, blaring in the sudden hush of a pricklingly cold night, came from my near left.

We were intertwined, and I didn't know which parts were mine and which were his. But now I knew what crash test dummies feel like. Tuppence chose that moment to stick her surprisingly warm nose in my face, accompanied by a short whine.

"Not hardly," I groaned. "Are you?" Air seared into my gasping lungs.

"No." But the word was shaky and pinched.

I rolled to my side and slowly pulled in my legs until I was kneeling. I brushed snow off Burke's face and chest, quickly ran my hands over his arms and legs. "Where does it hurt?"

"Everywhere. Nowhere." He awkwardly pushed up on his elbows, and squinted at me. "You're bleeding."

"Yeah. Sorry." I swiped my sleeve across my mouth, realizing a moment later that I was dripping crimson blops onto the pristine snow.

"We've gotta move," I whispered around my swelling lip and growing awareness of pain—dull, knotted pain in several locations I didn't want to think about.

"I know. But still, that was *awesome*!" Burke grunted as he scooched onto his knees.

He is such a boy. In other circumstances, I suppose we should've taken a moment to appreciate our daring feat—and that we'd survived.

Instead, I gingerly pulled him to his feet, and he seemed steady on them. For the first time, I swung my head to look back up the hill, and there they were—two men in dark clothing sliding downhill sideways in the track we'd made, their foot placement making them look like tentative snowboarders standing out in relief against the bluish-white background.

They wouldn't be tentative for long.

"Up and over the berm," I said. "The riverbank is rough with big boulders. It's our best chance at having cover."

"I know. I already explored here. I was going to hop an eastbound train on this side while it was still going slow from crossing the bridge." Burke tested his first step, and began to climb.

I had nothing to add to that revelation, except to note with an incongruous burst of brief hopefulness that it was phrased entirely in the past tense. Maybe he was no longer considering carrying on with his solo sojourn. Besides, I had no ability to speak, as I, too, was clawing my way back up the berm, grabbing whatever stout weed stems and stray, denuded blackberry brambles I could for balance. I only noticed the thorns piercing my palms in a surreal, abstracted way as my hands developed traces of reluctant blood.

"Don't linger," I huffed as we neared the top. "Straight across."

Again, my warning was unnecessary, but isn't nagging the parental thing to do? To stand upright on the railroad berm would be to make ourselves clear and stark targets.

My hands and knees sunk through the snow and grated on the rough cinders and railroad ties tacky with creosote even in the below-freezing temperature. On the other side we rolled again—it was the fastest way to get down to the rugged shoreline.

Tuppence was becoming a nuisance—and she'd be a liability if she continued trailing us.

"Scram!" I flung out my arm, trying to urge her away, my voice firm and hoarse, and far too loud in my own ears.

But she didn't believe me. I never raise my voice to her; it had never been necessary. So she just stood still on stiff legs and cocked her head at me expectantly, her tail slowing in its exuberant arc but not stopping completely.

She is, after all, a dog, and completely failed to see what isn't fun about a nighttime dash through the snow and undergrowth.

I knelt and grabbed her head in my sticky hands. "Go home," I rasped. "Find Pete. Go!" And I gave her an encouraging whump on the hindquarters.

Whether she understood me or not, she wheeled and dug into the steep snowy side of the berm, gamboling up it in great bounding leaps that flung sprays of ice particles.

Burke was tugging on my hand again, and we turned toward the rugged barrenness of the riverbank. Rocks bigger than cars piled in a mishmash, looming silent and foreboding in the eerie glow. I had no idea where the light was coming from, but it seemed trapped in an endless, reverberating reflection from the low underbellies of the pewter clouds to the snow-swept crust of the earth and back again.

We slipped into the nearest crevice and slid carefully, feeling the rough, ancient volcanic jags with our fingertips and toes, seeking sure footing. There were gaps big enough to lose a leg in, not to mention rib-cracking landing pads should we fall, and the near guarantee that we would wrench ankles or break wrists if we stumbled.

It was a twisty-turny maze with tight spots that snagged at my coat as I inched myself along. Burke was faring better, being smaller. As soon as we could hear the water lapping and gurgling around the rock we were standing on, we angled right—west, downriver.

The *Surely* was docked not too far away—if you're counting in miles, at highway speed—at the Port of Platts Landing. It would be a long and arduous trek the way we were doing it, primarily with our scraped hands, knees, elbows and clinging with tenuous toeholds, but she was there at the end of the line and we might possibly be able to seek shelter in her narrow galley.

"Wait, wait." Burke groped for my arm in the dark. "Listen."

Water tinkled and plunked and blurbled cheerily underneath us with a lightness that made me think ice was accumulating up in the sheltered spaces between the rocks. Luckily, we hadn't slipped on any ice patches yet.

"There," Burke breathed. "Hear it?"

Indeed, I did. It sounded like my name. My very own name, being shouted in duet. No, trio. Quartet? A couple female and a couple male voices.

But one voice made my heart flutter, on top of the pounding it was already doing. The voice was Pete's. And he was hollering my *entire* name. *Meredith Marie Morehouse Sills*. So that I would know, beyond a shadow of a doubt, that it was him. I don't trust my middle name to just anybody, as I'm sure you can understand. I'd learned that lesson by the second grade when I was called

3M in taunting, sing-song voices by enough treacherous schoolmates to last me a lifetime.

The other thing that struck me—so deeply that I keeled, panting, against the nearest boulder from the mental impact—is that they were calling *only* my name, not Burke's. Which meant they suspected the murderers were still within earshot.

"Hold on." I grabbed the back of Burke's coat before he could turn and give away our hiding spot.

Our approaching rescuers were making a lot of noise. On purpose. Piercing whistles. More shouts. And finally, Tuppence, adding her mournful, yipping howl to the mix.

I released Burke when we spotted the first bobbing flashlight beams. "You can move now, slowly toward the berm. But don't speak. I'll answer them."

I wished I knew how to whistle, but I don't. So my hoarse voice would have to do. "Okay!" I shouted. "I'm okay!" Singular. Just in case.

"Stay where you are!" came the answering command. In Sheriff Marge's deep, no-nonsense bellow, the one she uses to tell criminals to get on the ground, spread-eagle. You don't argue with a voice like that.

So Burke and I eased ourselves down to sitting positions against the comforting bosom of a massive boulder, making sure we were below the sightline from the berm to the river.

"Talk to me, Meredith," Sheriff Marge shouted. She was getting closer now, trotting along the top of the berm, judging by the short jerking progress of the closest flashlight beam. Apparently *she* wasn't worried about presenting herself as a target.

Another flashlight beam was rapidly gaining on Sheriff Marge's. "Babe!" he shouted.

My man. My insides just about melted with crushing happiness, and I whimpered. My eyes were suddenly swimming, blurring the sharp edges of the boulders around us.

Burke wedged his arm through mine and tipped his head against my shoulder. "It's okay," he whispered. "We're gonna be okay. They won't get to you the way they hurt that other lady." He was stroking my arm, petting me, clinging to me, and his little voice was thick with emotion. "You won't die. Not like that."

A gut-wrenching sickness of understanding washed over me. Flooded my soul until I couldn't breathe. Because now I knew *why*. Why he'd been so insistent, so fierce, so determined to get me out of the house. He was protecting *me*.

To make up for the last time, when he hadn't been able to save Cassidy.

A burden unfathomable.

CHAPTER 22

Pete didn't like it—letting Burke and me out of his sight—but he drove the pickup, with Tuppence riding shotgun, and hugged Sheriff Marge's bumper, at speed, all the way to the hospital in Lupine.

Because I hadn't been able to laugh off the appearance of my lip and hands or the splatters and smears of blood I'd left behind on the snow. Apparently, other people get touchy about these things.

Tuppence, also, had a couple shallow knife wounds—one on her flank and another into her left shoulder—which we'd discovered most belatedly because she hadn't let on one bit, instead prancing around like her normal, eager self. Perhaps even more animatedly than usual when she showed us her treasures—a fleece-lined man's glove and a woolen knit hat. In the dark, it'd been difficult—with her black and white spotted fur—to see that she was bleeding too.

Sheriff Marge had promptly bundled the articles of clothing into padded evidence bags—snapping on latex gloves of her own before she did so—and bundled Burke and me into her white and green Ford Interceptor sport utility vehicle with the county logo on the sides. In the back, behind the wire mesh. But that way Burke and I could stay together. He'd become positively clingy in the aftermath of our flight, and so had I.

Hester Maxwell drove the third vehicle in our little convoy. She'd been the first to raise the alarm and had a deeply vested interest in the outcome. Sheriff Marge warned her the coming proceedings might take all night, and she hadn't batted an eye, instead climbing into her old, battered Honda Civic and revving the engine. She had studded tires on the front-wheel-drive car, and she was having no difficulty in keeping up with Sheriff Marge's edge-of-the-seat-gripping pace.

"I see they released you," I said through gritted teeth from behind the security bars.

"Passed that sucker," Sheriff Marge agreed from the front seat. "Size of a small pea. You should've seen it."

Actually, I'd take a pass on that sort of voyeurism, but didn't say so out loud. Instead, I said, "Shouldn't you be taking it easy?"

Which earned me a hard glare from steel-gray eyes in the rearview mirror just as she navigated a sharp curve. Burke and I were slung across the seat—just our upper halves since we were cinched at the hips with seat belts—and enjoyed a double-whammy smash against the far door as first I hit and then Burke hit me.

"You're bleeding all over the place, and you have the gall to ask me that?" Sheriff Marge fired over her shoulder as we whipped around another, mirrored, curve in the serpentine scenic highway. This time I landed on Burke.

Maybe it wasn't a good idea to talk back to Sheriff Marge when she was pushing triple digits on the speedometer and her siren was blaring.

She squealed to a whiplash stop in the pull-through entrance to the hospital's emergency room and popped the locks on our doors with a secret switch she had in the front.

Burke tumbled out of the vehicle behind me and nearly face-planted on the pavement. "Wow," he breathed as I helped him regain his footing on solid, unmoving ground.

"And you thought the cardboard-flyer ride was the highlight of our evening," I muttered.

Burke just shook his head and patted the gleaming side of the Interceptor. "I've gotta get me one of these," he said with an impish grin.

I might've made a ticklish jab at him through his puffy coat—all in good fun, of course. "Not until you're sixteen, at least," I said in a gruff tone while failing to keep my own grin off my face. Just fulfilling my end of the nagging-parent bargain. "Forty-six would be better," I added.

"Try fifty-eight," Sheriff Marge said, bustling around from the driver's side. "That's how old I was when I took the driving course at the Washington State Patrol's training facility." She hesitated for a fraction of a second mid-stride, and glared at me. "What are you standing here for? You're not so beat up that you need a gurney. Get yourself in gear." And she marched on toward the automatic sliding glass door.

"I think they put something extra in her IV," I murmured to Burke.

"I heard that!" But she didn't stop to lecture me further, and Burke and I had no choice but to follow behind.

Once inside, Sheriff Marge continued her stiff power walk straight to the women's restroom while Burke and I were immediately surrounded by people in scrubs.

And by one nurse who eschewed the comfort of elastic-waist pants and still ascribed to the old-school starched white blouse and skirt. "Fluids," Gemma explained as she gripped my arm and led me to a semi-reclined lounge chair covered with a narrow strip of sanitary paper.

Just like the comforts of home—not. The paper crinkled and tore and stuck to me as I scooted my fanny onboard.

"She's under strict orders," Gemma continued while pinching back one of my eyelids and peering into the deep recesses of my eyeball with her luminous, pale green eyes. The strength of the correction in her burgundy-framed cat's-eye glasses magnified her eyes to near-alien size and gave her an omniscient aura that was more than a little disconcerting. "To prevent future kidney stones, Sheriff Marge has to hydrate extensively," she said matter-of-factly, and then she swabbed the crook of my elbow with a cold alcohol wipe.

Well, that explained quite a lot.

~oOo~

It was a night of special circumstances in the emergency room. Our presiding doctor, a young—but apparently very game—man who had "Dr. Lipscomb" stitched above the pocket of his lab coat, decided there was no need to roust the veterinarian, Doc Corn, from his Monday night poker game, and that since Tuppence's wounds were fairly superficial, he could do the stitching himself—once he'd finished with me.

"I don't suppose you have Cheez Whiz?" I mumbled dubiously, thinking of Doc Corn's magic trick of squirting a long line of the creamy cheese-like substance on his stainless-steel exam table to keep my greedy canine otherwise occupied while he engaged in the more unpleasant aspects of a check-up. My mouth felt like cotton, and my lips weren't functioning properly, swollen as they were, with a small, discrete bandage taped across the lower one where I'd punctured it.

Tuppence seemed absolutely oblivious to the fact that she'd been injured, and instead was giddy with delight at all the people paying attention to her in this new place full of interesting smells. But I was worried her attitude might change as soon as a stranger started poking her with a needle.

Gemma held up a finger. "I have one better." She sailed off, the starched skirt of her uniform snapping in her self-created breeze.

She returned with her lunch—or perhaps more accurately defined as her midnight snack, given the shift she was working—a peanut butter sandwich.

I started to object, but she fluttered a dismissive hand. "It's for a good cause," she asserted, and there was no arguing with her, either.

Sheriff Marge was filling the gap in the privacy curtains, her arms akimbo, glaring tolerantly at the melee, kind of like a bouncer at a bar—a nice bar where they hand out painkillers and ice chips and antiseptic creams. I might've been a little loopy, but it was also at that moment that I realized I was far outnumbered by highly experienced, bossy women, and all attempts at asserting my own will would be thwarted.

Hester, one of the guardian trio, had taken position in the hard plastic chair placed squarely between my paper-protected lounge chair and Burke's. She was knitting furiously, stabbing at the fuzzy blue wad in her lap with both needles.

Pete was perched on the edge of a hard chair on my other side, tenderly balancing one of my bandaged hands between his own, not saying anything. But there was a seriousness to those sapphire-blue eyes and creases at the corners of his mouth that meant he was thinking, analyzing—and not about pleasant things.

My mind needed to go there, too, but I wasn't sure I was quite ready for that harsh of a reality check. So, I turned to Hester. "Can we take a mulligan on the interview?"

"No need," she huffed indignantly. "Believe it or not, I had a good look around your house and your accommodations meet all the criteria. I was a little early, and your back door was wide open, so I let myself in," she added, unapologetically. "But I knew something was dreadfully wrong when I spotted the bottle of Windex sitting in the middle of the living room floor."

"I'd been cleaning," I explained meekly.

"Everyone does," she replied curtly, "when they know I'm coming. My very presence is anathema to grime in this county." She said this with a tinge of perverse satisfaction and a tight smile. Her eyes were backlit with a sort of sarcastic glee that had me responding with a grin of my own.

A grin that hurt. I winced, and reapplied the ice pack.

And caught Burke watching me. He had scrapes and bruises, but no injury that required more than washing with hydrogen peroxide and a couple Band-Aids. He'd been plied early and often with hot cocoa, and while he gave the impression of contentedly slurping from the current Styrofoam cup, the eyes behind his tangled fringe of hair held a grim, indecipherable expression. They were almost mirror images of Pete's in their seriousness—just in a different color.

I gave him a lopsided smile, no longer caring how much it hurt. When could he go back to being a regular kid? I yearned for that—for him, with a sudden, rushing palpitation in my chest. I had to crack open my mouth to breathe.

"Then I realized your front door had been jimmied open." Hester was still talking, stabbing the wool in her lap with renewed venom. "Why they didn't sidle around to the back, I have no idea. It was prudent to assume, then and there, that they were trying to sneak up on you. Sheriff Marge had given me a bit of the backstory, you see. Coming through the front door would, indeed, take most Sockeye County families by surprise," she added, more to herself than to me.

Sheriff Marge had eased closer, her notebook out, her pen poised, overtly eavesdropping, with an agenda.

Hester didn't seem fully aware that her audience had expanded as she sighed and flipped her knitting around to purl back. "I'm quite sure I passed by their car on the way in. A gray—or maybe black—Acura. It was parked in the last camping spot, closest to your house, but not really visible from the house in the dark. Black on black, as it were."

I'd gasped at the mention of the car, and cringed involuntarily the moment it slipped out—because I should've known better. Should've paid attention. Now all eyes had swiveled to me.

"I realize there are a lot of gray Acuras out there, but I saw one too—on Sunday night, behind the museum. No one was inside," I offered in feeble defense.

Sheriff Marge was glowering and scribbling furiously, but she didn't berate me for my lapse. "License plate?"

I shook my head. "From Washington, but I didn't get the number. I figured it was left by a guest from the wedding reception. Maybe mechanical problems, or..." I shrugged.

Sheriff Marge turned those gray spotlights onto Hester, but the social worker also had to shake her head. "I didn't get the number either. The car was no longer in the camping spot when we left, so that strengthens my opinion that the two men fled in it."

Sheriff Marge was already on her cell phone, holding a stunted, monosyllabic conversation with the person on the other end of the line, and ferociously contemplating a spot on the wall above my head. She wasn't liking the answers she was hearing.

She heaved a frustrated gust when she clicked off the call and shoved the phone back into one of her many pockets. "Dale and Owen already found the tracks and footprints in that spot. Said it was G-39."

She pitched her brows at me, and I nodded. G-39 was, indeed, one of the spots closest to the house in a full hookup loop. It was usually one of the last spots to get reserved in the summer, though, because it didn't have an unobstructed view of the river. Instead, it was nearly ringed by upstart pin oaks and scraggly huckleberry bushes, affording privacy in lieu of expansive scenery.

"The snow won't hold the prints," Pete contributed quietly, almost startling me. Other than the warm strength of his hands around mine, I'd forgotten he was sitting there, stewing.

"Right," Sheriff Marge grunted. "They're taking pictures, which is all they can do. But it's already too late. We weren't going to get anything useful from those, anyway."

"The hat and glove?" I queried.

"Those are good," Sheriff Marge agreed, but then added a caveat that crushed my little surge of hope, "if the wearer is in the system. I hate to admit it, but these guys are smart. And patient. That combination—which is so rare in common criminals—is never something I like to see."

"So they're not common." Pete said. "That, in itself, will narrow the field."

Sheriff Marge was nodding along. "Motive. We know why they're after this young fella here"—she tipped the brim of her hat toward Burke—"so we need to keep hard on the line of enquiry about why they felt they had to get rid of Cassidy."

"Her secrets—which she didn't know herself, most likely—are hidden with her equipment," I murmured. We all knew; I just felt like saying it out loud again.

"I expect they've been destroyed by now." Sheriff Marge is a stickler for the facts—and the reasonable conclusions that should be drawn from them—no matter how discouraging they might be. She doesn't tolerate fairy-tale dreaming.

Dr. Lipscomb stuck his pink-cheeked baby face around the curtain and spoke with an accent that was much more southerly-leaning now that he wasn't issuing medical assessments and directives. "You all are going to have to move your conference elsewhere," he said. "An elderly man has fallen off a roof, and we're about to get really busy in here in a few minutes."

"In this weather?" Hester clucked. "What was he thinking?"

But Sheriff Marge's gaze had snapped up sharply, and she pinned Dr. Lipscomb with it. "Who?"

"I can't...well..." he stuttered. "It's my duty to protect the privacy of..."

But Sheriff Marge's right eyebrow had reached the apex of dictatorial supremacy, and Dr. Lipscomb quailed under her glare. Good thing my tidy bandage hid my wincing smirk. The young upstart would soon learn which side his bread was buttered on.

"Uh, Ira Cupples," he conceded, flushing hotly. Then he quickly clarified, "Senior."

If Sheriff Marge had been an eye-roller, she would've done so now. "I thought so," she grunted instead. "Keep him heavily sedated. I can't afford to make another emergency run back here tonight to defuse some kind of hostage situation. Don't let him anywhere near your scalpels or needles. And don't let him fool you into thinking he's some sort of feeble, spacey old man. You got that?"

Dr. Lipscomb revealed his good breeding by snappily and rotely responding, "Yes, ma'am." He nearly saluted.

CHAPTER 23

We reconvened, after traveling motorcade-style yet again, at the sheriff's department's modular building. The sagging structure is perched on concrete blocks in the middle of the crackled and potholed parking lot of an abandoned supermarket. The county had purchased the property with grand plans for a new law enforcement complex, but somebody had forgotten to tell the accountant how much the proper facilities would cost to build from scratch. The good citizens of Sockeye County, and much more so her sworn peace officers, were waiting for the economy to turn around, and the tax base to rise commensurately, so they could finally build an office that didn't smell like mildew and scorched frozen burritos and a jail that had electronic locks on the cell doors and separate accommodations for men and women. In other words, a brave new world. Or maybe just joining the twenty-first century.

Patience is a virtue everywhere, but it's a matter of remedial survival when you live in the sticks. That, and an extraordinary tolerance for discomfort.

As proved by the way Sheriff Marge's deputies were sprawled over and behind their cluttered desks—assembling, collating, and organizing the disparate facts they'd collected that evening.

Archie Lanphier was standing by a printer that was groaning in a perfect imitation of death throes as it jerkily ratcheted out a single sheet of paper. "Got the Acura," he said as we shuffled inside, stamping the slush off our shoes.

The visitors' seating area consists of one garage-sale-reject lime-green couch with self-esteem issues. I nudged Burke toward it, and settled in beside him— *settling* being the operative word. I sank until my knees were nearly level with my chin.

But I was suddenly exhausted beyond description and didn't care about my ungainliness since the cushions were the kind of soft and clumpy squishy that indicated their interior foam had disintegrated decades ago. My eyelids began drooping of their own accord—probably also a symptom of adrenaline crash.

There was room on the couch for one more, but Pete chose to lean against the door frame, his hands jammed in his jeans pockets, silent and scowling.

Nadine, the dispatcher and office manager, and who probably should've gone home ages ago, took one look at Burke and jumped up from behind her desk. She's a firm believer in foundational support of the unmentionable variety. And, apparently she's in the right profession, because the shape of her brassiere is what's commonly known as a bullet bra, the likes of which haven't been seen in public since the late 1950s—except on Nadine. She has torpedoes on her chest. Nothing jiggled.

I was tempted to slap a hand over Burke's eyes. Except, well, the searing damage was already done.

"You want Pop-Tarts, hon?" she asked in a throaty smoker's voice. The offer was clearly aimed at Burke only, and I suspected that Nadine, also, had been primed with enough of his backstory to have developed a few spastic maternal twinges for the hard-case orphan.

"No," I snapped, instantly zapping into hyper-alert parent mode. "But thank you." The kid was going to float away from a hot cocoa overdose as it was. I wrapped an arm around him, and he leaned into me.

Snuggled, actually. Nestled, his shaggy hair tickling under my chin, and a flood of conflicting emotions just about smothered me.

Hester gave Nadine a withering glare, and she strode across the room between us as though she was drawing an imaginary—but very real—battle line. She yanked the top chair off a stack of plastic spares and plunked into it like the resolute chaperone she was. As a ward of the state, Burke's psychological condition and sweet tooth were as much her responsibility as they were mine, and I was grateful for the backup.

Nadine sniffed and wiggled her loose-jointed hips back into her own seat.

Sheriff Marge had come in last, and just caught the tip of Archie's statement. "Where?"

"Stolen out of Kennewick three days ago," Archie replied.

Sheriff Marge is the only person with a private office in the stubby little module, but she eschewed it in lieu of the corner of Nadine's desk, where she hitched her broad backside after wrangling the equipment dangling from her duty belt out of the way. "The only one?" she asked.

"Yup," said our taciturn deputy.

"Not too many of those to choose from in these parts." Sheriff Marge nodded stiffly. "Our perps are showing some surprising consistency. Doesn't help us much, though, since it's still consistency we can't trace back far enough."

I had my mouth open to ask for clarification, but Sheriff Marge beat me to it with a new train of thought. "Before we go any further, Pete—" She rose and went over to the coffee station. She tore open a packet of herbal tea and set about dunking it methodically into a cup of hot water. "I know you've already given your complete statement to the Gilliam County sheriff's department, but I'd like to hear it in your own words."

My head was on a swivel between the herbal tea and Pete. Caffeine-free? Statement? Dual shocks to my system at the same time. It wasn't like Pete and I'd had time to have a marital tête-à-tête since the tobogganing incident, but what hadn't he told me?! And what on earth was Sheriff Marge drinking?

Pete's blue eyes bore into mine for a long moment before he turned to Sheriff Marge and complied with her request. "I got a call from Delbert Mason, out in Arlington, Oregon this afternoon."

Heads were nodding in the room, along with a couple grunts of recognition from the deputies. Apparently Delbert Mason was well known along both sides of the river. A man who manages a port that includes a grain co-op and elevator usually does hold that sort of status.

"Said he wanted my opinion on a project he was considering. It's not the first time he's asked me, so the request—while the timing was a little odd—wasn't completely unusual, so I went." Pete shifted, pressed his back more firmly into the hard ridges of the door frame, and his scowl tightened. "When I got out to the port, Del's truck was the only vehicle in the parking lot. Again, not unusual, especially this time of year. I went straight up to his office; the door was barely latched. It swung open under my knock. And there was Del, strapped to his office chair with duct tape, a gag across his mouth."

My eyeballs about popped out, and I made a strangled little gurgling noise.

Pete shot me a worried glance, but continued. "So I cut him loose. I was concerned about fingerprints—if I was smudging over ones that might've been left by the people who did that to him—but he told me, as soon as I got the tape off his face, that the men had been wearing balaclavas and gloves, that they'd been very careful to cover their tracks. They hadn't even spoken to him. They'd written out their demands on paper ahead of time, including the reason he was supposed to give me on the phone to get me to come out."

"Now that's something." Sheriff Marge grimaced as she slurped her tea—from the heat or the insipid flavor, I couldn't tell. "I think we can assume from the written communication that the perps knew Del would recognize their voices if they spoke—why they had to completely mask their identities. What weapon did they use?"

"Del's not sure. They jabbed something in his back, which he assumed was the muzzle of a gun, and they smacked him with something hard on the back of the head when he put up some resistance, but he never saw the weapon."

"But he saw the car?" Sheriff Marge prodded. Apparently she'd read the full report, and just wanted to cement the details into her mind.

Again Pete's tone was grim. "Not to fully identify it. He spotted it from his office window, coming down that steep, winding road into the port. He said it was black, one of those Japanese jobs. You know Del—if it's not American made, he has no use for it. And he's certain he doesn't know anybody who owns a car like that."

In the far corner, Dale Larson chuckled shortly and wagged his head from side to side. "One of the perks of using a stolen vehicle. Our boys are bright."

"Yeah. But they're desperate," Sheriff Marge retorted, her eyes narrowing behind the reading glasses as though she was seeing a far-off vision.

Everyone in the room seemed to hold their breath, waiting. She was working on something. Calculating. Applying her extensive knowledge of human nature and criminal behavior.

She heaved a sigh and balanced the barely sipped cup of tea on the edge of the table. "Here's how I see it," she said finally. She was squinting at me and Burke, but the intensity of her glare softened. She crossed over to us in two steps and bent to ruffle his hair, kind of pawed it away from his face for a second, held his gaze, and gave him a curt nod. "They don't like you much, Burke." She squatted down so she was at eye level with him. "I was hoping those two men would show themselves, and also hoping they wouldn't, because of the possible consequences of that. Are you understanding me?"

Burke's head rubbed against my shoulder as he nodded.

I wasn't quite sure I was following as closely as I needed to be, but I dug my fingernails into my thigh and tried to focus.

"They seem determined to get you, because your ability to identify them is very important," Sheriff Marge continued, speaking straight to Burke. "The sketches you helped Ms. Oliphant produce are very helpful, but there are lots of ways for a good defense lawyer to get around those in court. They're not definitive, not sufficient in and of themselves. To shift the preponderance of evidence, we would need to produce *you* as an eyewitness to be sure of a conviction."

A lot of big words, each one like a blow straight to my gut. I'd known this, of course, even consciously as well as subconsciously, in all the deep recesses of my brain. But hearing the confirmation spoken in Sheriff Marge's solemn voice made my hands tremble.

"The fact that these men didn't just disappear, didn't just go back to their normal lives hoping that you'd forget or that maybe you didn't see too much that day in the forest—well, it scares me too."

"I can be brave," Burke whispered.

She thunked his leg with her knuckle in an approving manner. "You already are. No question about that. But I'm going to ask for more." She pushed to standing with some alarmingly loud pops in her knees.

"I don't like what you're thinking," Pete said from the doorway, his voice grating with strain.

She turned slowly to face him, then kept moving, her gaze returning to settle on me. "I don't like it either."

CHAPTER 24

Sheriff Marge did give Hester the chance to pull the plug on her plan. But Hester puffed up like an indignant mother hen and stated forcefully and clearly that it was her official opinion, on behalf of the state, that the sooner this whole ordeal was over, the better for the child. His life was in danger, and would continue to be so, until the two killers were behind bars.

So I was outfitted with a Taser and given cursory instruction on how to operate it. While I was trying to wrap my head around *aim with the laser sight at bare skin or thin clothing over areas of large muscle mass* (unlikely in this weather)—*prong connect—electrical conduction—silence is golden, a loud buzzing noise means try again or if he's too close just jab the guy with it for pain compliance,* I noticed that Owen Hobart had dropped to one knee beside Burke and they were having what appeared to be an intense conversation.

It was the first time Owen had spoken since we'd arrived at the station. He's a man of few words, but the ones that do come out are worth listening to. Burke nodded vigorously several times and even responded verbally, but I couldn't hear what either one of them was saying. Owen's big hand rested on Burke's shoulder briefly before they split apart.

It was nearly midnight, but I was exhausted well beyond the fact that it was past my bedtime. My bones ached.

We rode home in the pickup, with Pete driving. My head tipped against his shoulder, and Burke had slumped against me, domino style. Tuppence had been snoozing in the cab, and she grudgingly made room for us.

Now I understood my husband's preoccupation, his sullen scowling all evening, and the gritty fury that was still shimmering off him like a heat-fueled mirage.

I waited until both Tuppence and Burke were snoring softly. "Why didn't you tell me?" I whispered.

He had to clear his throat before he could speak. "At first, I didn't want to scare you. I knew you'd be busy getting ready for Hester's interview, and I thought if I was lucky, I might be able to get home in time for that and just walk into the house like nothing was wrong. I called Sheriff Marge. She put the scenario together a little better than I did—the full import of why I'd been called away. So then I did try your phone, as I was racing back here, but you weren't answering." His hand gripped my knee in the dark. "That was the most terrifying hour of my life, babe. I didn't get to you in time." His voice was thick, almost slurred.

I buried my face in his shoulder. "You can't shield me from everything."

"I can try." His hand tightened on my knee.

I tilted my head up, squinted to see his profile in the dull glow from the dashboard lights. "I don't want that. I want all of real life, no matter how much it hurts. Because I also want the fullness of joy that comes with the pain. Okay? I want to *know*."

"Then you know I love you."

I could only nod, tears had clogged my throat.

~oOo~

The general consensus had been that the killers wouldn't try again—at least not immediately—to reach Burke at the Sills' house. But their tactic with Delbert Mason and the way they'd stolen at least two vehicles from locations where they had good chances of getting away with it indicated that they were familiar and comfortable with a broad range of territory and with people's habits.

It was clear the perps didn't mind being up-close-and-personal with their victims. They were neither squeamish nor afraid, nor easily flustered. They'd been extremely hands-on, whether for murder or just intimidation. And, so far, they'd avoided the actual firing of a gun, although they had to be considered armed and dangerous.

Sheriff Marge thought—given how careful the killers had been about not leaving evidence behind—that they would be very wary of shooting, because of the bullets, spent casings, and possible gunpowder residue. Everything leaves a trail. Now that she had the hat and glove and possible DNA samples from those to match with any deposits they made in the future, they'd have to be even more circumspect.

She was banking on a battle of wits, otherwise she would never have asked Meredith and Burke to take the necessary risks. Owen had to agree with her. The sooner the better. Trap them at their own game. But that didn't mean he wasn't on edge.

He was also no longer envious of Pete. He couldn't imagine placing his wife and a young boy who was officially under his protection out as bait for two clever killers. But, as Sheriff Marge had pointed out, they were bait whether anyone wanted to acknowledge that unpleasant fact or not. Might as well spring the bait in the right trap.

Owen had gone home after the meeting and donned his old-school cold-weather gear, this time with a layer of camouflage on top. Then he'd driven his personal vehicle—a beater pickup that looked like every other beater pickup in the county—to the Port of Platts Landing and hiked over to the old Tinsley homestead where the Sills family were pretending everything was normal.

His first shift assignment was to keep watch, from a distance, unobtrusively, just in case. He hadn't wanted the boy to worry or panic if he was spotted in his gear, lurking among the trees, so he'd taken a few minutes to explain before they'd all departed. And to drop a few hints about life in foster care, life without one's original parents. Owen knew all about that. Knew all about new parents who could turn out far better than the biological set. Or not. But he'd promised Burke that the best place to live in the whole county was with Pete and Meredith. If anybody had extra love to dump on a kid like Burke, it was them. He'd be safe there. Lots of people were looking out for him.

Still, he wasn't surprised, in the wee hours of the morning, when all the lights on the upper story of the farmhouse snapped on, one by one. Mostly the blinds were drawn, but there were cracks and gaps of light, and the small window in the bathroom was ablaze. Then the kitchen light came on, and he saw Meredith's shadow at the sink. It was another nightmare—had to be. You can give a kid all the assurances possible during the day, but once his subconscious takes over, during sleep, the irrational monsters emerge. Owen knew all about that, too. Knew all about the reasons kids have nightmares.

He still did, sometimes, but for grown-up reasons now, for Afghanistan reasons. Came with the territory. And he wasn't at all sure how a woman like Darcy O'Hare would react to that kind of issue.

But he'd made the call, as instructed. He always followed orders when they came from true superiors. And he figured Frankie Cortland knew what she was talking about in that department. She was a woman, after all. The maternal sort. Bossy. Demanding. He'd known he was being manipulated, ever so unsubtly maneuvered into a certain course of action, but he'd gone along with it.

Because maybe a woman like Darcy was worth it. Maybe. She'd been agreeable—they had a date planned. Preliminary mission accomplished. Provided his current mission didn't extend into the following weekend. Yet another reason to catch those two bastards quickly.

So he prowled, crept through the trees in a deep semicircle around the house, arcing back and forth, rifle at the ready, watching the entrances, eyeing the front door where he and Dale had screwed a sheet of plywood to the door frame to cover the wrecked lock, learning the Sills' patterns. He'd have to see and recognize the unusual things, the anomalies, if he was to be ready, so he could protect them when the moment came.

And it would come, he was sure of that.

~oOo~

My job was to keep up appearances. With Burke in tow. That sounds like it ought to be simple. And it is, in theory. But you try acting normal when there's a very good chance a pair of creeps who'd already murdered one defenseless girl and knocked around a middle-aged man, essentially kidnapping him in his own office, might be looking at you through binoculars, might be shadowing your every step.

I'd already committed my first deviation from the norm when I retrieved the clippers from the shelf in the upstairs closet before breakfast.

"Trims," I announced when the males in the household came downstairs. "Both of you."

Pete didn't really need it, but I hoped that having a role model would encourage Burke to shed his tangled mop with few complaints.

Not that the boy complained about anything.

He sat quietly while I buzzed the clippers over his head in the utilitarian one-length-everywhere style. He looked about three years younger when I finished, and his eyes were hollow behind their brightness. All three of us were ghosts of ourselves after the previous harrowing day and very short night.

When I swept the resulting dead animal's worth of hair out the door, I thought I saw Owen, or somebody with Owen's broad physique, out in the trees. Almost like he wanted me to know he was there.

I nearly waved, out of habit—and then didn't, in case anyone else was watching too. Owen's presence was reassuring. The idea of anyone else's was disturbing—and terrifying.

Breakfast was a silent affair, as if we were sleepwalking through the motions. Even Burke seemed to have lost his appetite.

Until, in a voice that held a curious note of triumph, he pointed out, "You haven't kissed this morning."

"You're right." Pete set down his coffee mug and skeptically eyed the bandage on my lower lip.

I cast a quick wink at Burke, and suggested to my husband in a husky whisper, "I have other places that are kissable."

Burke exited the kitchen like his scalp was on fire. He made no secret of his stomps up the stairs, either.

Pete was chuckling deeply as he nuzzled into my neck. "We're going to have that kid well-trained in a matter of days."

"Don't bet on it." But I was grinning under Pete's attentions. How I craved normalcy.

~oOo~

"Where are you?" Sheriff Marge growled into the phone.

"In my office."

"We need you acting normally."

"This *is* normal. In case you forgot, you asked me to develop an exhibit on the history of crime and punishment in this county. And that requires *extensive* research." I drew out the word, and Burke offered a slight grin from his cross-legged position on the floor where he'd been hand-drawing a time line for our exhibit, those mineral-green eyes even more gigantic now that they weren't shaded by overhanging hair. He looked positively unearthly with his grayish pallor and stubbled head. I hadn't done him a fashion favor with the new coiffure.

"You need to find a different kind of normal. One that gets you outside." Sheriff Marge was sounding positively grouchy. She had every reason to be, of course, and I actually found her gruffness reassuring, but I was beginning to wonder if an exacerbating factor was the lack of caffeine. In her newfound zeal to avoid any future kidney stones, she'd taken to glugging copious amounts of barely flavored warm water and therefore trotting to the ladies' room every half hour. Not fun when you're also on a roving stakeout. Although she was most certainly not a complainer, I'd been catching hints of her travails in the form of very regular, pestering phone calls.

"Go for a walk," she continued. "It's nearly lunch time. Finney's down at the Burger Basket & Bait Shop, checking the floats for damage after this last storm. I can get him to fire up the grill for you."

"Wouldn't that seem out of character?" I asked.

"Just do it." She clicked off before I could object further.

She was right, as always. I was just cringing in the back of my mind, knowing that the moment I stepped outside the safety of the Imogene's thick walls, the little boy with me would have a target on his back. No—I had to correct my thinking. The target had been there from the moment he'd witnessed Cassidy's murder; it just became easier to hit when he was exposed. Which was the whole point of this exercise.

I struggled into my coat and helped Burke with his as well. The Taser was clunky and awkward, jammed into my coat pocket.

Outside, we were greeted by the Big Slush. This is not an official weather-forecasting term, but it's still highly accurate. We'd worn rubber boots to work, and with good reason. The sun had emerged, with all her cheerful heat, and she was busy evaporating our frozen precipitation into the splatty stuff. Rivulets of water were trickling and gurgling down, through, and under the rapidly diminishing snowbanks in a misleading prelude to the suggestion of a spring thaw.

We'd left Tuppence at home. We'd had to. She would've introduced yet another unpredictable variable into our already congested situation. Sheriff Marge and her deputies were attempting to contain and monitor all possible contacts with us, so they could winnow out the two men they were hunting. But my hound would've loved diving nose-first into the muck and digging her way back out.

As it was, Burke and I splashed across the parking lot, squinting against the brilliant, reflecting light. I could barely see a few feet in front of me for all the glare, so there was no opportunity for surreptitious scanning of the horizon in hopes of catching glimpses of our protectors.

Finney, clearly, had received advance notice of our arrival, and he was whistling tunefully through the big gap between his front teeth as he rummaged in a large stainless-steel clad refrigerator.

"Yoo-hoo," I called to his backside. We'd clumped through the eating area of the floating restaurant and were waiting for permission to enter the hallowed space behind the serving window.

"Yup," Finney hollered back. "Pickings are slim, but I could rustle up some grilled cheese sandwiches for you two."

"Finney, you've been closed since October. The fact that you can produce any food at all makes you my hero," I replied.

"Then you might not want to look at how much mold I'll have to scrape off the cheese." Finney backed out of the fridge and let the door whump closed behind him. His freckled face broke into a wide grin, and he kept straightening to his full, and very scrawny, height. "Well now, you must be Burke." He offered a big paw for Burke to shake. "Heard about your plight."

That had been another one of Sheriff Marge's brilliant reversals of strategy. Use the townspeople to protect Burke too, since she had limited paid resources, and there was no way she and her deputies could personally cover every avenue. But when all the shopkeepers and civil servants and farmers know to keep an eye out for two men, whose sketches have been provided—but not posted—they wouldn't get very far before the warning phone calls would start rolling in.

It was a fine line she was walking, because if the murderers realized they were being sought, actively, by a whole town, they'd quite logically not come anywhere near us again. The trick was to draw them in for another attempt on Burke without making it obvious.

Burke seemed enamored—or awed—by the bustling Finney. It was probably related to the way Finney moved acrobatically about the gleaming kitchen, whipping up lunches with what appeared to be disjointed abandon but also remarkable efficiency. Finney had learned to cook in the Navy—he could've probably fed a thousand sailors with only a minimal increase in his energetic output.

But it wasn't until he plunked three loaded plates down on the stainless steel counter in front of us that I knew he'd been more than forewarned. Someone had made reservations for our lunch, maybe even hinted that the shop needed a winterizing review to start with.

Sheriff Marge strode in through the side door—the one that led directly from the floating walkway where fishermen tied their boats in the summer, essentially the restaurant's back porch. I had no idea how long she'd been lurking out there, but she was dressed for the slush in padded ski pants and a bulky jacket and a knit cap pulled down tight over her ears—the second time in my life I'd seen her in civilian clothing.

"I'm burning up," she said, stopping between two long tables where the chairs had been upended on top of them to ease floor mopping. She shed several layers and draped them over airborne chair legs to dry.

"Any activity?" I asked.

"Nope. This waiting could go on for a long while." She hitched a hip up onto the stool next to mine and nodded her thanks to Finney.

Burke had already inhaled half his sandwich, a small packet of salt and vinegar potato chips, and requested a refill of his orange Crush pop. Making up for his lackluster breakfast, no doubt.

I groaned. "You don't have the budget for this."

"Nope. The guys are all waiving their overtime rates. They're also waiving sleep, and that's the more serious problem." Her eyes were rimmed with a bluish-purple that indicated she should've included herself in the sleep-deprived category as well.

"What can I do?" I murmured.

"Carry on." She shook her head. "Just carry on. Owen's picking at an idea, and it's a valid one. But it won't be quick."

"What idea?"

"SeedGenix."

Finney whistled softly as he slid plates of apple pie adorned with Butter Brickle ice cream in front of us. The man is a magician. "You're gonna ruffle some feathers."

"Don't I know it." Sheriff Marge sighed and slid her mug over so Finney could refill it with hot water. "But it's the only common denominator. Owen has reconstructed Cassidy's last two weeks as best he can, but there's a huge gap when she went missing. Her absence wasn't reported right away because it wasn't unusual. As an independent researcher, she had a lot of flexibility in her schedule, but she'd been doing some shadowing of scientists at the major seed companies when she had the chance, even took a trip to the Midwest over Christmas break on her own dime—she's that interested in their developmental wheat tests. Or in keeping her patrons happy—academic research is a weird and conflicting mix of funding sources. The only seed company out here on the west side of the country is SeedGenix, and her research—what we know of it—seems like it would dovetail nicely with the company's goals. Owen's gone out to their headquarters to have a look around."

Finney's eyebrows arched over his freckled face in an expression of concern that made me stop nibbling around the edges of my sandwich. "Unofficially?" he asked.

Sheriff Marge's lips pursed, and she weighed her answer for a moment. "Quietly," she conceded.

So it was political, this nosing about. Not directly, but the company was too big and too important to the local economy to risk upsetting its management, or board of directors if it was publicly traded. Touchy. I didn't envy Sheriff Marge one bit. She didn't have a lot of influence in the matter because SeedGenix wasn't physically located in her territory.

I don't like waiting. I'm not sure I've ever met anyone who does. But waiting under stress, waiting under uncertainty, waiting under threat? That'll wear a person's soul down to the nubbins.

CHAPTER 25

For the past forty-five minutes, Owen had been parked on the edge of a gravel road, the sun glaring across the windshield of his old truck as it sank toward the horizon, with his elbows propped on the rim of the open driver's side window while he squinted through his field glasses. He was judging the time and distance between himself and the white speck of a 4 x 4 that was cruising toward him at a speed a little too fast for comfort on the potholed track. The Franklin County sheriff's logo stood out in relief on the 4 x 4's door. Somebody had called him in, no question about it.

Because he was glaringly obvious, the exact opposite of the techniques he'd employed during the surveillance duty he'd pulled at the Sills' house—out of necessity. Frankly, he was surprised that it had taken this long for someone to become suspicious. In Sockeye County, Sheriff Marge would've been called *before* a pickup parked in the same spot at the same time three days in a row.

There was no place to hide. No trees. Out here on the eastern side of Washington, the topography was a lot flatter, and a lot browner underneath the skiffs of crystalline snow. You could see for miles and miles. Especially with a good pair of binoculars.

He returned his attention to the bleak parking lot surrounding SeedGenix's headquarters building on the outskirts of Pasco, Washington. Neat rows of cars baking in the weak winter sunlight, their paint oxidizing to chalky powder. It'd get bitterly cold the moment the sun went down—a dry sort of hacking cold that seemed to numb the whole town into somnolence. Or drunken mindlessness.

He should know. He'd spent the past two nights moving from tavern to tavern, having noted and followed and plotted the routes of at least twenty different cars from the SeedGenix parking lot at quitting time. About fifty percent of the employees seemed to go straight home, to spouses and kids and split-level ranch houses with respectable yards and mortgages. They weren't the people he wanted to talk to.

Hence the taverns and the jukeboxes and the desperate women clamoring for his attention, thick as thieves, clinging to his arms and begging him to dance, laughing boozy breath in his face. His stomach roiled at the thought of another night spent working his way through a series of awkward conversations and confrontations with extremely reluctant employees once they realized he wasn't at the bar for a good time. Ms. Oliphant's sketches hadn't gotten him anywhere, yet.

What he needed was someone disenfranchised, someone whose entire livelihood wasn't contingent upon their job, preferably someone without dependents. Someone whose moral conscience wasn't biased by pecuniary considerations. Those people were hard to come by.

He'd just about memorized the SeedGenix web page that showed the portraits and positivity-enhanced bios of department heads, but he'd probably need to corner a lowlier, rank-and-file employee. But it'd have to be the right rank-and-file employee, someone who knew something *and* was willing to share the information.

Because all the SeedGenix information he'd been able to find in the public domain was full of corporate speakeasy language—big, optimistic, future-expanding words that promised little and apparently satisfied the legal department's strict censure. Promises that couldn't be pinned down. Forecasts with prevailing loopholes. A whole lot of nothing concrete.

His idea was such a long shot that he was a little surprised Sheriff Marge had let him pursue it this far, this long, when the department was stretched as thin as it was. She'd shared his intuition, though. Probably because it was a variant of the old standard—follow the money.

Two minutes to quitting time—the SeedGenix parking lot was about to suffer its daily mass exodus. And he didn't want to make that approaching sheriff's deputy think he was leading him on some sort of cowboy car chase.

The engine in his pickup turned over with a reliable chug, and he eased his foot off the brake. An orderly retreat, two minutes out, then he'd be mingled in with the departing stampede from SeedGenix and pick out his next mark.

~oOo~

She was frumpy, and she was grocery shopping. Two entirely promising traits.

She bought her clothes from one of those stores that does all the color coordinating for you and sells complete outfits instead of individual pieces. The clunky beads in her necklace were the exact same shade of dusty-orange-pink as the oversized flowers that cascaded over the left shoulder of her cardigan like a big, fake corsage. Her pointy patent shoes, more appropriate for sitting in an office than for tromping through a dark, icy parking lot and into the climate-controlled Muzak of Smithers' IGA, were dyed to match. It was a uniform of sorts, nearly regimented enough to compete with his usual khakis, or any of the uniforms he'd worn in the Army previously.

For the first time, he felt underdressed and a bit awkward in jeans and a waxed canvas field coat. He wasn't going to hit on her. Not that he was any good at flirting, anyway.

She just didn't seem to be the sort that would be flattered by attentions from a younger man. Not that he had any experience in that regard, either. But the weary peckishness that characterized her demeanor—and the selections she was tossing into her cart—hinted at a response of sheer incredulity and quite possibly a sarcastic fit of giggles if he approached her that way. Or, even more possibly, a karate chop in the nuts.

He held the shopping basket in front of him as he angled closer. He was just going to tell her the truth. Then she could wallop him, if she wanted to. Or scream. Or whatever.

That Franklin County deputy had gotten pretty close in the stream of cars exiting SeedGenix—he had to assume his license plate number had been checked and cross-referenced and that Franklin County now knew they had an out-of-jurisdiction deputy from downriver nosing around, one who hadn't bothered to place a courtesy call to their chief just yet. Sheriff Marge had warned him to be circumspect and discreet because SeedGenix's tentacles were mighty long.

Ms. Frump might be his last foray in attempting to recruit an informant before he was reeled in for questioning himself. "Hello," he rasped. He cleared his throat and tried again. "I'm Owen. Owen Hobart."

Her head snapped up, and she glared at him narrowly. No sound was going to escape from those thin lips which seemed gummed together by the remnants of dried-out lipstick—in that same pinkish-orange shade that reminded him of vomit.

The kind of vomit that occurs after you've eaten too much strawberry rhubarb pie. That was another vivid memory flash—actually, one of the happier ones—from his collection of experiences with all the foster families he'd been pawned off on as a kid.

Owen shook his head and reaffixed his gaze, directly into her eyes, and vowed not to let it slip any further south to that disturbing color. "I'm a deputy sheriff from Sockeye County. I understand you work at SeedGenix." He had his hand poised over his pocket, loose and ready, should she demand to see his badge and identification.

Without meaning to, he'd dropped his voice another notch when he'd said the company name. That alone, all by itself, made her eyes—they were a nice, cool brown—widen. She paused for a fraction of a second, not moving any more or less than before, still glaring, but he could see her thinking, analyzing, weighing something. And then she nodded—once, short and to the point.

Owen exhaled. Set the basket on the floor and carefully slid two papers out of the opposite pocket. He unfolded them and smoothed them out on the broad sides of the cereal boxes on the shelf beside him, holding them up as though they were pinned on the Most Wanted board.

He didn't have to say anything. She was already peering closely at the drawings, leaning over the handlebar of her shopping cart.

Then she raised her own hand, and held it horizontally over the knit cap on the head of the man Burke had described as the *boss*, blocking that portion of the drawing from her view as though it distracted her.

She nodded again, that single sharp movement, and straightened. She blinked at him, and finally said, quietly, "I think you'd better come for supper, young man. I assume, since you followed me here, that you can also follow me to my house." It was a statement, not a question. She wheeled her cart around and resumed chucking things into it haphazardly.

~oOo~

Her name was Charlotte Vraible, and she was a terrible cook. Actually, she didn't cook at all—she thawed and reheated. Chicken pot pies were on the menu. Owen accepted that offer, mainly because they would take at least forty minutes before they were edible, and he needed that time with her, to pick her brain. But he did turn down the offer of a pinkish-hued white Zinfandel which she tapped from a spout in the foil-lined box in the fridge.

"I had to invite you home," she stated matter-of-factly after her first, apparently soothing, sip. "I had to sign non-disclosures up the wazoo just to get a job interview with SeedGenix. Then another whole layer once they hired me. I can't be standing, chatting about them, in the cereal aisle at the market. You know how it is."

Indeed he did. "Can you chat about them now?" he asked, glancing around her kitchen, which still sported dull goldenrod linoleum and dark cabinets waxy with decades of grease deposits. The walls were speckled yellow, and not because they'd been painted that way.

She had to think about it for another intense half-minute. Then she countered with, "Is this about that girl? The one who was killed?"

Owen nodded. "You know?"

She blew out an exasperated breath. "Everyone knows." But then she shrugged. "Maybe me more than most around here. My son is a senior at WSU this year. The news is all over campus. Can't hide something like that, even if you wanted to." She was studying him carefully, waiting.

So he nodded again, and opted for the truth again. "It's a fine line, in police work, deciding how much of the investigation to reveal. Which details will help us catch the killers and which would help them get away, or enable them to concoct confirmable alibis."

"And you think they have—or had—something to do with SeedGenix."

"So do you." She wouldn't have invited him into her home if she didn't.

"This all has to be anonymous," she said suddenly, setting her glass on the countertop with a click. "I can't have my name associated with anything I might tell you."

"You have my word. I just need help getting on the right track. Then I'll do the legwork."

For the first time, a slight smile curved her lips. She'd been pretty, once. Owen was guessing she was divorced, and not amicably. She carried bitterness around like a cloudy aura. It was obvious she lived alone. Not even a cat to keep her company.

He stayed for two hours, and mostly he talked. He ate the pot pie without even noticing if it tasted like cardboard or not. She queried him closely and in so much detail that he began to think of her as a prosecuting attorney. There was very little he held back, only a few questions where he had to give a terse "No comment" reply.

"The problem is that I know I've seen him"— Charlotte flicked a hand at the sketches Owen had flattened on the dining table between them—"but I can't place the situation, the context in which I've seen him. Which makes me think I've seen his picture, and not him in person."

"But he works at SeedGenix?" Owen prodded.

"No. Definitely not. It's actually a small company, and I know everyone on the payroll. The headquarters building mainly houses the administrative functions, the sales teams—when they're in their offices and not out on the road—human resources, accounting, that sort of thing. It doesn't house the brain trust of the company." She gave him a wry, weary smile. "You don't know how this works, do you?"

Owen could only shake his head.

"The science, the genetic modifications, the testing—all the research—is done by an indistinct and sprawling network of contracted scientists, many of whom run their own labs and collaborate or not as the whim or funding strikes them. There are a lot of strong personalities involved who don't necessarily get along with each other. Scientists are a bristly and territorial bunch, rife with competition. That's why they have to sign lock-tight contracts and reams of non-disclosure agreements in order to get funding from the company. SeedGenix wants to own the results, but they don't necessarily care how those results are obtained as long as no one talks about it."

"So each scientist, or each lab, could possibly be working on projects for competing companies at the same time?" he asked.

"Oh, yes. Guaranteed. They likely wouldn't be able to earn a living otherwise. They're expected to compartmentalize and have the paperwork to prove it."

"And if they don't?"

"One—or all—of the interested companies will sue them into oblivion for breach of contract." Charlotte shrugged. "It's happened. The companies have insurmountably deep pockets."

"And our guy?" Owen gestured toward the boss, whose angry eyes were staring from the sketch.

"He's connected with one of the labs—I'm quite sure. I may have even processed payments for him. I handle all of the accounts payable, everything from the monthly utilities to the multi-year research grants. His name has definitely crossed my desk." Her chin was propped on the heel of her hand, and she absently traced the copy of Ms. Oliphant's graphite marks with a fingertip. "Or the name of the lab he works for, but I feel like it's his name, that maybe his name is part of the lab's name. Eponymous," she murmured.

CHAPTER 26

You don't wake somebody at 4:17 a.m. for a social call. Owen knew what this was. It was a low-key dawn raid, conducted when he would be at his weakest and most vulnerable. It was just disguised as concern for a brother-in-arms.

He stood in the crack allowed by the chain on the cheap motel door and squinted at the two deputies silhouetted by the high-beam headlights of their patrol vehicle which were shining directly at him. They were all armed, and they all knew it. Nobody was pulling a weapon—nobody was flinching.

The Franklin County deputies were protecting their own and not-so-subtly clarifying their opinion regarding his continued presence. As messages went, it was quite distinct, no matter how couched it was in fake bonhomie. They had people and businesses to watch over, and were territorial in their own right. He would've been upset if one of them had been stalking Sockeye County residents the way he'd been after their own people. It was fair, but that didn't make it pleasant.

"The sheriff wants to see you in his office at eight," the heavier-set one said. "Just to shoot the breeze. Nothing serious. You on vacation?"

"Yeah," Owen lied. "Thinking about transferring out here where it rains less. Got any openings?"

The skinnier, shorter one whose hat was backlit like an eclipse in the high-beam snorted, then spat. Chewing tobacco on the job. "You kidding? There's been a hiring freeze for three years."

"Could be a lateral, take the place of a less qualified deputy. I'm sure you've got plenty of those." The insinuation wasn't even that—his threat was glaringly obvious, and they didn't like it much. Owen grinned to himself. It'd taken them nearly four days to pinpoint his location when he wasn't even hiding. Sloppy. And this early-morning wake-up call was even sloppier.

The fat one pointed at him. "Eight o'clock. Sharp. The old man doesn't like to be kept waiting."

Owen closed the door with a thud. His boss didn't like to be kept waiting, either, and his mission here was as complete as he could make it under the circumstances. Might as well pack up and head out. It wasn't like he was going to go back to sleep. And it sure wouldn't hurt the sheriff of Franklin County to be stood up.

~oOo~

Her call came at 10:34 a.m. Breathless, furtive, muffled—it sounded as though Charlotte was crouched under her desk, speaking in a hoarse whisper.

Owen sincerely hoped she wasn't calling attention to herself with unusual behavior as he veered sharply onto the gravel shoulder of State Route 14 and brought his pickup to a sliding halt. There was no one behind him, hadn't been for miles, so he wasn't creating a traffic hazard. He put his flashers on anyway, circumspect in all things, and pulled out his notebook.

"You okay?" he asked.

"Yes," she hissed. "I'm down in the janitor's supply closet. He's been pilfering for a while, but following up on his inventory now is the perfect cover for the other unusual records searching I did this morning."

Owen wasn't shocked, but he was a little surprised that the tactic of holding the pursuit of misdemeanor crimes in reserve as cover for deeper investigations seemed to apply in the sanitary white-collar world just as surely as it did in the law enforcement world. Perhaps he'd underestimated Charlotte. "Are you feeling threatened?" He just wanted to be sure. She was a nice lady, for all of her crustiness, and she didn't need another hardship in her life.

"Not at all," she huffed. "Just easier to talk in here without being overheard. Besides, the sheriff is in the building this morning, in conference with our general manager. Consequently, everyone's ears are pricked and twitchy. Cubicleville, you know. There are absolutely no secrets in this place."

"What time?" Owen asked.

"What time *what*?" Now Charlotte's voice was echoing a bit, probably bouncing off the concrete walls and metal shelving units in the janitor's draconian preserve as her volume increased.

"Shhh," he reminded her. "What time did the sheriff arrive?"

"Oh." Charlotte sounded taken aback. "Um, I'd say shortly before nine. He's still up there, as far as I know."

This new information was putting his wake-up call by committee in a new light. And made him even more glad he'd decided to skip the forcefully suggested invitation to meet with the sheriff himself. Who was in bed with whom? It was an interesting question.

Instead, Owen asked, "What did you find?"

"Nothing," Charlotte squeaked. "And that's just the point." She was speaking faster, either agitated or excited.

Owen decided not to interrupt, let her get it out, whatever it was. And quickly, so she could get back to her desk and start acting normal again.

"I went through all the research contracts by reverse order of due date," she whispered, "figuring that whatever led those men to murder Cassidy must've been somewhat urgent."

Owen nodded along, agreeing with her logic, and doodled in his notebook to keep himself from expressing the impatience that was building inside his chest. Arrows. Arrows were always good for indicating the direction both information and money flowed.

"And then I went to the websites for the labs that have contracts with SeedGenix, just to get a feel for what kind of work they might be doing, to look at the pictures of their staff. They love to do that, you know, put up professional portraits that make their labs look good."

Just like SeedGenix's own site, Owen thought grimly. It's irresistible, that urge to splash your face all over the place when you're an uppity-up. Something no street-level law enforcement officer would ever, ever, ever do—not if he valued his own life or those of his family. And especially not if that family included a woman with iridescent copper-red hair and incredible curves. He shook his head abruptly and fought to bring his attention back to the words being whispered into his ear.

"I found him by *not* finding him," Charlotte continued. "And it's eponymous, like I thought."

"Back up," Owen blurted, scribbling for real in his notebook now. "Who? And where?"

"It's an outfit called Truitt BotoTechnologies. Get it? *Botany* and *technology*? Their mailing address is in the next town over—Kennewick. The main principal is Gordon Truitt, and his number two, the head of research, is his brother-in-law, Russ Herren."

What a difference a few miles made. Both Kennewick and Pasco were part of the metropolitan area known as the Tri-Cities, but they were in different counties, separated by the Columbia River on the north-south(ish) stretch of her run near her confluence with the Snake River, and therefore had different sheriffs in charge with very different perspectives on what, exactly, community-oriented policing means.

"The men match the sketches?" Owen wanted to be absolutely sure.

"No." Charlotte rushed headlong into her explanation. "Their photos are gone. I'm sure they were there on the website before and everyone else who holds a title at the lab does have a photo up on the website, but not these two men. I think the photos have been removed, and recently, even though their bios are still viewable. But I did some more digging, looking for news articles online, reports in the local business journals, anything. I found another grainy photo of the two of them as part of a chamber of commerce technology task force about ten years ago. It's them!"

Owen's phone vibrated as she sent an email with the website link. He clicked through, but she was right— the image was incredibly grainy, low resolution, something that had been printed on newsprint originally. He was going to have to blow it up on a larger screen, and then maybe even run the pixelated result past Ms. Oliphant and her keen eye for facial structure.

"Every other lab website you looked at seemed intact?" he asked. "No gaping holes like this one?"

"Right." Charlotte's voice was thick with satisfaction. The needle in the haystack—she'd found it. A case of guilt by intentional omission. Maybe.

"Thank you." Owen meant it.

"Just, you know...get them," she whispered into the phone. "Killing a young woman, a student. My son..." She breathed heavily. "A few variances in the situation, and it could've been him who was murdered to cover up whatever it is they're hiding." And then she added the clincher. "Well, if science can't be transparent, then what? We base our whole lives on the research and reports these labs produce—the food we eat, the water we drink. What if they're not true?"

She was a woman who loved her facts. A woman after his own heart. "Be careful," he reminded her. "Try to be around people this weekend, in public places, but nothing too much outside of your normal routine, either." He shook his head, grimacing at the conflicting instructions which would be impossible for her to follow completely.

She laughed softly, but the acidic edge he'd come to expect was missing from her words. "I'm a woman of a certain age, with an attitude. I'm sure you noticed. I'll be fine."

This whole scouting trip had always been a long shot, even from the very beginning—especially from the very beginning. He dialed Sheriff Marge's number. She deserved to know that she might've, by proxy through him, made an ambitious enemy of the Franklin County sheriff. And she could get on the two scientists' names quicker than he could while he was still on the road.

"What's happening?" he asked as soon as she answered.

"Nothing. Zilch. Nada," Sheriff Marge grumbled. "We're all going stir-crazy, Meredith and Burke most of all. Pete's about to pop an artery, trying to protect them without seeming to protect them. No one's sleeping. Tell me you found something."

So he did.

"Let's hope you and your source are right," Sheriff Marge replied. "There've been fourteen road-licensed vehicles stolen in Franklin, Benton, Yakima, Klickitat, Umatilla, Morrow, Gilliam, Sherman, Wasco, and Hood River counties since those two men put in an appearance at the Sills' place on Monday night. I'm sending you an email with the list right now. I suspect they're in one of those vehicles, since that's their MO."

Owen noticed she hadn't included Sockeye County in the list, which meant no vehicles had been reported stolen in his home county in the intervening days—not unusual. But she'd included all the bordering Oregon counties between Pasco and Platts Landing, meaning she thought the murderers might hop across state lines if it suited them. They'd done it before, presumably, when they'd strapped Del Mason to his office chair over in Arlington. They definitely knew the lay of the land.

"Got it," Owen confirmed. "You're watching the bridges?" There were only five along that nearly 200-mile stretch of river, serving as man-made choke points for vehicle traffic.

"The Oregon counties' sheriffs' departments are covering them on their side," she said.

Again, he drew a breath of relief. That meant the Franklin County sheriff wouldn't be involved in that part of the operation. It's not great to have a potential antagonist covering your rear. Depending on the personality of a sheriff, those elected officials could come to view their counties as big, sprawling fiefdoms. He was lucky to work for one who didn't have an inflated ego.

Sheriff Marge seemed to have read his mind, because she kept talking, "Don't worry about old Ronnie. I know his wife pretty well. He's not running for reelection next time around, so he's not going to do something stupid and risk having a big mistake become his legacy. He'll play by the rules, even if he doesn't like it much."

"Would he warn off previous big campaign donors? Out of loyalty?" Owen queried.

"*What* loyalty?" Sheriff Marge might've cackled a bit. "I'll give Pearl a call, just in case. She wears the pants in that household, no matter who has the badge. Now get back here as quick as you can."

CHAPTER 27

I was becoming complacent. I knew it, and that worried me almost more than the original threat. Because nothing was happening. Either the two men who had chased us out of our house had saintly amounts of patience (how would that even be possible?), or they'd taken off for parts unknown. I detested the ambiguity of our situation.

I was just about out of publicly visible but not-very-approachable tasks to do around the museum, too. It was January, after all. The time when all reasonable people are at least semi-hibernating, leaving their houses only to do the necessary shopping and runs to take their kids somewhere or go to work. Only the most die-hard outdoor recreational enthusiasts and out-of-season hunters were traipsing about the countryside. People like Cassidy, I realized with a sickening knot in my stomach—the ones who owned cold-temperature mummy bags and Gore-Tex everything else.

So it was with some reluctance that I'd mentioned to Burke at breakfast that our next project would be cleaning out the Imogene's former kitchen garden and marking off new plots to plant in the spring. I'd been dreaming of doing this for some time. The problem was that the Big Slush had turned into the Big Muck as far as the garden was concerned. But it made sense to knock down the rotting gazebo while we were at it.

I wondered when Burke had last gotten a tetanus shot. He hadn't come with much verifiable provenance and definitely without an instruction manual. But he was keeping up a cheerfulness and a work ethic that endeared him to me and broke my heart at the same time. As though maybe he felt he needed to earn a spot in our family.

Apparently sledgehammers and crowbars provide a delightful level of novelty for young boys. Burke's face was flushed with exertion, and his eyes shone with enthusiasm. The support posts for the gazebo splintered easily under our thudding swings, and the roof lurched sideways before keeling over in what looked like a dead faint—an undramatic climax that was more about wormhole-riddled pith than proper deconstructive engineering on our part.

In an hour, we had a nice pile of fragmented wood that would be useful only as kindling. But after the close call with an arson fire the past autumn, there was no way I would allow a bonfire. I'd hire Jim Carter to come out with his little front-loader and shift the gazebo's remains into a dumpster—when the ground was firm enough to support the weight of his machinery.

In the meantime, Burke and I could get a head start on those raised beds for vegetables, herbs and flowers. "Supply run," I announced. "You'll like this place. They have a pretty good candy aisle."

~oOo~

There was something bugging him. Well, something bigger than all the other pressing problems racing through his mind. It had taken thirty miles for him to scratch through that mental cacophony and identify the irritant.

Fourteen stolen cars in four days. Fourteen *reported* stolen cars in four days. But there were more—there had to be. The farms in all these rural counties often had extra vehicles scattered on their land, specifically for field use. In winter, it might take weeks, or even months, before a truck that'd been parked behind a barn would be noticed as missing. Plus there were the parking lots at the little regional airports where a vehicle might've been intentionally left for a stretch of time. Hikers parked at trail heads and disappeared for days, fully expecting their cars to still be there when they returned.

The murderers would have a lot of vehicles to choose from. Or they might even use their own personal vehicles—if they estimated they had a good chance of success for a second attempt on Burke.

So, just pulling a number out of the air, Owen assumed the possible list of vehicles to be on the lookout for would be two, even three, times that original fourteen. Too many to be effective at watching for, especially when you didn't know which ones they were. And if the killers were smart, they wouldn't choose an Acura this time. He considered that to have been a major slip in their clever planning.

He'd watch for the vehicles on the list—of course he would. It was the best he and his fellow deputies could do.

But the truth was, those guys could be anywhere. He'd feel better if he could eliminate some places where they *weren't*. He skidded into the parking lot at the base of Beacon Rock—he needed to use the facilities anyway, stretch his legs, place a call or two.

Sheriff Marge hadn't asked the Benton County sheriff to go out to Truitt BotoTechnologies and nose around. Because she couldn't—not based on what little evidence they had. Reasonably, the connections Owen had winkled out of Charlotte couldn't even be called *evidence*. They wouldn't be able to get a search warrant for the property or an arrest warrant for Truitt or Herren based on one grainy photo and Charlotte's speculative assumption, which was itself based on her impression of artist sketches. The chain linking the men and events wasn't strong enough to persuade a judge.

Which is where social engineering came into play. Maybe. He'd never done it before, but he'd taken a course on the few related laws and huge, currently unlegislated, gray areas surrounding it.

Owen blew out a big breath and punched in the number for Truitt BotoTechnologies. Who knew—maybe Truitt himself would answer the phone and put the kibosh on all these wild assumptions.

But no, it was the chirpy voice of a young female in a greeting she must repeat a hundred times a day. She mashed the name of the lab together so fast, he wouldn't have recognized the rapid-fire words if he wasn't already aware of the number he'd dialed.

"Can I speak with Gordy?" Owen asked, keeping his tone light and hoping madly that Truitt's friends used that nickname for him. In the back of his mind, he was quickly slinging together some ambiguous backstory that he could call upon and that also wouldn't be an outright lie.

But the perky receptionist made all his conniving unnecessary. "Nope, sorry. They're gone again."

"They?" And *Again?* he wanted to ask, but thought it prudent to keep to one question at a time.

"Dr. Truitt and Dr. Herren." Her tone had deepened, become a bit wary.

"Rats. Are they at the conference out in Omaha?" Owen snatched a major Midwestern city out of a handful of choices. He'd never been there, but he hoped it sounded realistic.

"No," she said slowly. "Backpacking. They left yesterday around four."

Not the answer he'd really wanted to hear, but it was the one he'd been fearing. "You're sure? That's a lot of playing hooky." He took another chance with the offhand, casual remark, trying to build some common ground with the receptionist.

"Of course I'm sure." She'd turned slightly snippy. "I saw them leave, didn't I? Besides, I would've made their travel arrangements if they were flying anyplace or needed hotel rooms booked. No, they've gotten this sudden urge to test out their cold-weather gear in preparation for some trip they're planning to Alaska. Crazy, if you ask me. But it gives them the excuse to take long weekends just when the rest of our technicians are working overtime to meet the second phase trial deadline for—" She caught herself in the nick of time and swerved into the generic, "well, for one of our clients."

Ah, employee dissatisfaction. He'd been the beneficiary of that sentiment twice now in the past twenty-four hours. In his gut, he knew now that Truitt and Herren's out-of-office time would match up with their extracurricular activities related to Cassidy and hunting down Burke. Sheriff Marge could get a search warrant for their work calendar when the time came.

His immediate concern was to get out of the call gracefully, without piquing the receptionist's curiosity.

He'd used his personal phone—it could be traced. "Some guys have all the fun," he said, commiserating.

"Well, all that time off doesn't make them any more cheerful, that's for sure," she huffed. "They've been impossible to work with the past few months. Demanding and sullen, and really, really suspicious, like they think everybody's out to get them. I'm thinking of quitting."

"Maybe you should," Owen offered. "Change of pace, change of scenery." How much more bland could he get? Did she want platitudes, or advice? He needed to hang up, but not memorably. "Look, I gotta go," he blurted just as she started to respond with another complaint. "I'll catch up with the guys later."

"You wanna leave a message?" she asked hopefully.

"Not this time, sweetheart." He clicked off.

He did, indeed, have a lot of catching up to do.

CHAPTER 28

Driving to the hardware/household goods/craft supply/drugstore in Lupine was an adventure in normalcy. The loose security net Sheriff Marge and her deputies had formed around us was always there, but I couldn't always spot them, since they'd been swapping out their personal vehicles for others of unknown—to me, at any rate—origins. Good tactics, and that probably kept me from giving away their presence by staring around for them too much. Relying on them too much.

But constant vigilance was wearing me down. Pete, too, although he'd never complain. And Burke as well, although it was hard to tell just how much the stress was getting to him, except in the food consumption department—that *had* waned a bit. Maybe I'd finally filled him up.

But candy is candy is candy and seems to have its own separate gastronomical compartment. The kid's eyes were alight as we slowly worked our way down that particular aisle. Cracker Jack boxes, clove-flavored chewing gum, Necco Wafers, Idaho Spud candy bars, Charleston Chews, Life Savers in flavors I hadn't seen in decades. It was a walk down memory lane, and a real effort for me to refrain from tossing one of each into my cart.

"You can pick out three things you want when we come back through," I said, more for myself than for Burke. "But let's get the bulky stuff first."

The store was bustling with shoppers. There was an air of mild exuberance at being released from the previous constraints of snow and ice and a general level of optimism and do-it-yourselfism, judging by the contents of the carts we passed. They were brimming with everything from toilet paper to gaudy fake flowers to hand saws to gallons of paint to toasters to duck hunting decoys. And one giant stuffed panda bear with its proud new owner-to-be twirling along in her mother's wake, dressed in a sparkly pink tutu over thick leggings and cute rubber boots that were colored to look like green frogs. Something for everybody, clearly.

Ralph Moses was at his usual station behind the pharmacy counter, and I wondered if he'd made any progress in his wooing of Betty Jenkins due to Frankie's and my propitious seating arrangements at the wedding reception. I made a mental note to ask for an update and lifted my hand to wave to him before Burke and I pushed through a side door into the store's roofed outdoor enclosure that doubled as a garden center in the summer.

The exterior metal gates were locked for the season, restricting access to the single doorway from the store as a shoplifting prevention method. The laissez-faire attitude of most retailers in Sockeye County had sharpened with the latest spate of vandalism, and reasonably so. Compared to the usual security measures at stores in urban areas, they'd been remarkably lax in the past. No longer.

Burke and I, each pushing our own squeaky-wheeled cart across the lumpy pavement, headed straight for the pallets of mulch, compost and fertilizer at the far end. They were leftovers from the previous planting season, but they'd suit my purposes.

"What about this?" Burke slid a pitchfork-shaped implement off a nearby rack and held it up for me to see.

I nodded. "Looks effective. And one of those hoes, too," I added, pointing. "We already have shovels and rakes, but we're going to need stakes and a big ball of twine, and that pH soil tester thingy," I said, pointing again, the novice directing the utterly inexperienced. I was grateful we had the enclosure to ourselves, and there wasn't an audience for my green-thumb uncertainty. Nobody else seemed tempted to browse garden supplies in January.

Burke was quickly filling his cart while I manhandled ten bags of organic steer manure into mine— and, eventually, onto the bottom rack of his cart as well.

It seemed crazy to be paying for gourmet cow poop, but I did want the thoroughly sanitized stuff. I'd heard the horror stories about fly infestations stemming from improperly sourced fertilizers. I couldn't think of much worse than having swarms of insect hatchlings buzzing museum visitors in the spring should they choose to picnic on the grounds near the lush garden I had envisioned. But the old garden plot had been dormant and neglected for a long time, and it needed all the help it could get in the form of soil amendments.

We wrangled our overloaded, balky carts into a mini train and began the slow procession toward the door, the obstinate wheels objecting vociferously every inch of the way. I was in the middle, pushing my cart and helping to pull Burke's, while he constituted the caboose, also pushing for all he was worth, when I noticed a large, lurking form next to the wheelbarrow display.

He rose out of a crouch and grabbed me, clamping a hard hand over my mouth before I could yell out.

But Burke did. "Help!" he immediately shrilled in a voice that belied the size of his body. "Help!"

"Shut up," the man growled. "Or she gets it." He flashed a blade in front of my face, so close I couldn't focus well enough to see what type it was.

His short beard was grating on my cheek like sandpaper, and he squeezed his arms around me like a python. He swung me up off the ground and redeposited me hard after a half-turn, cinching my back up tight against his chest so that we were both facing Burke and all three of us could see the knife—a nasty serrated number that was longer than my hand.

I was staring at Burke, my eyes nearly popping with the effort to will him to continue yelling, but he'd snapped his mouth shut at the man's instruction, so tightly that his lips were white.

The Taser was in my pocket, but I couldn't reach it with my arms pinned. So this was what Cassidy's final minutes had felt like.

I wasn't going down without a fight, knife or no knife. Burke would need just a moment to get away, to start yelling his head off again.

I couldn't open my mouth far enough to get my teeth around one of the guy's fingers, so I poked my tongue out and wiggled it on his salty skin.

He was not one to be easily grossed out. He grunted and shifted my weight, pressing his thigh up under my bottom and almost lifting my toes off the ground. "Cut it out," he said. "Take it easy and you won't be hurt."

There was no way I could believe him. Especially since I knew they really wanted Burke instead. I'd just been easier to grab. And so far, I seemed to be a good bargaining chip for controlling the boy's actions.

Sheriff Marge was close, very close—I knew she was. Plus one or more of her deputies. Ralph had seen us, along with a lot of other shoppers who weren't necessarily paying attention. But maybe someone had heard Burke's first shouts?

How could I tell Burke not to worry about me, to just go—to run into the store and raise the alarm? He was rooted in place, his little chest heaving, his eyes so huge they looked like medallions.

My feet were still free—I could kick. So I did, aiming the rubber heels of my boots where I thought my attacker's knees would be, pummeling, and letting him hold my body weight.

His only option was to drop me—or to stab me, but the angle was bad if he wanted to avoid accidentally nicking himself. We were all dressed in thick layers of warm clothing, so I willed myself to think of the wool and puffy, quilted down as a shield, and jabbed out my legs one more time after I came down hard on my knees on the pavement. Then I rolled.

I rolled right up against the metal external gate for the enclosure and came to a stop staring up into the *boss* face from Ms. Oliphant's sketch. He, too, was growing a beard, but that aquiline nose and ridged brow were similar. The eyes were a dead giveaway—steeled and unrelenting.

He was outside the enclosure, but he held a pair of red-handled bolt cutters. In the fraction of a second it took to inhale a ragged, startled gasp, I wondered if people just drove around with bolt cutters in their trunks. The answer, in Sockeye County, was, unfortunately, yes. Not at all uncommon. Why couldn't we be normal and conveniently forget all the appropriate tools one might need in an emergency? Isn't that what AAA is for?

I could hardly fathom the fact that I was analyzing the situation in such depth. But my brain had been blocking some things out, and they now came raring back into focus with piercing clarity along with the pain that seemed to be radiating through my body from my knees upward.

Burke was yelling like a banshee and thrusting the pitchfork at my attacker, making him jig and scrabble over the toppled wheelbarrows while the glass door that led into the store exploded in a shower of splinters.

A tall man with broad shoulders and a raised rifle stepped through the broken door frame at the same time a voice I knew and loved shouted, "Sheriff! Hands up!" from over my shoulder.

I could weep for joy.

The only ones who didn't comply were Burke and me—well, and Owen because he wasn't supposed to. He was holding the rifle level and sighting down its length.

I failed to obey because I was already lying down and found that I was suddenly both limp and completely comfortable there on the ground, as if I'd been mashed in place with a steamroller. Also, I could sleep for days—just drop off for the next seventy-two hours or so.

And Burke because he was about to skewer the large man with the pitchfork. He had an expression of such virulent hostility on his small pale face that my breath caught in my throat. No child should ever look like that.

"Burke!" Sheriff Marge snapped. "Back off."

He did. Not easily, or quickly. But by degrees as the length of steel in his taut little body seemed to dissolve inch by inch until he dropped the pitchfork and crumpled with tears streaming down his face.

I pushed off the ground and lurched at him, scooping him up and swinging him away from the awfulness. I wrapped myself around him as best I could and wept into his shorn hair.

CHAPTER 29

There was a whole lot of hubbub. A whole lot of witnesses who'd seen tiny fragments of the proceedings and were anxious to give their statements. The arrests were most definitely a community affair.

Sheriff Marge had gotten three calls, one right after the other, just a few minutes after Burke and I had entered the store—two from customers in the parking lot about a suspicious truck stopped, but idling, around the back of the store behind the garden center enclosure, and one from a cashier who'd spotted the larger man, Dr. Herren, stride inside and then pause to carefully survey the entire store over the tops of the displays and endcaps. He'd been noticeable because all the local residents know exactly where the supplies they want are shelved; they don't need to read the hanging signs.

Deputy Dale Larsen had been our tailing protector from the Imogene into the town of Lupine, where he'd handed off responsibility to Deputy Archie Lanphier who was driving a borrowed Jeep Cherokee. Unbeknownst to me, Archie had entered the store just behind us, and he'd been feigning interest in the kitchen organizer section one aisle over while Burke and I drooled over the candy.

He'd been waylaid by a conversation. Just one of those polite, neighborly inquiries about life in general that he hadn't been able to get out of for about five minutes. Most of the townspeople knew that Sheriff Marge and her deputies were hunting a pair of murderers, but that didn't mean they were going to stop caring about the well-being of their friends, even if that friend was a deputy. And Archie had looked like he wasn't on duty, given his jeans and sheepskin coat and scuffed cowboy boots. Shopping on a Friday afternoon at the local everything store is the equivalent of social hour, and opportunities to catch up with acquaintances are not to be missed.

Archie hadn't wanted to draw attention to himself by being rude to the little old lady, and he'd seen us go into the garden center, which he knew would be empty in January. But he hadn't noticed the man with the new-growth beard following us until he realized the door into the garden center was barred on the outside with a couple long pieces of top rail for chain link fencing that had been wedged across from the racking on either side of the door.

Deputy Owen Hobart, on his way back from his out-of-town trip, had sped into the parking lot a moment later, and he'd taken up surveillance just inside the garden center door while Archie hustled all the customers and staff into the safety of the rear stockrooms.

Because that garden center? It would've been like shooting fish in a barrel. Again.

"They wouldn't have been able to escape if they'd shot you," Sheriff Marge reassured me, hours later. "Too noisy. Unless they'd used a silencer." She shrugged. "Which they didn't have. One gun between them—found it under the back seat in the cab—and it hasn't been fired in a while. Nope, they needed to keep their"—she paused, winced—"*removal* of Burke quiet, for a number of reasons. They still believed they could get away with it."

"In broad daylight, with so many people around?" I croaked. Our close call still hadn't fully sunk in. I was pretty sure I was going to get the shakes later, probably in the middle of the night, when the gravity of what might have been finally did pierce my thick subconscious.

Pete hadn't stopped touching me since he'd raced in from the port—Ralph had sheltered behind the pharmacy counter and called him during the scramble to shove customers to safety—and his arm was around my waist as we leaned against the bumper of our pickup in the nearly deserted parking lot. Burke was up in the bed of the truck with an extra blanket draped over his shoulders and Tuppence flopped across his lap. He probably couldn't have moved if he'd wanted to, but we were grateful and determined to keep him close. He was also listening to every word of our conversation, but there was no reason to pussyfoot around the situation, now that it was over.

"They were desperate," Sheriff Marge said grimly. "I haven't gotten the full story yet, but it's something about a genetically modified seed mix-up at their lab. Truitt's blaming Herren, and Herren's not talking."

"But Truitt's the boss?" I muttered. "He should know?"

"Exactly. He's culpable, both for the lab snafu, and especially for the murder, attempted kidnapping, attempted murder, vehicle thefts, what have you..." Her words trailed off at the litany of crimes. She went to lift her hat, realized it wasn't perched on top of her head since she was in plainclothes, and readjusted her reading glasses instead. "The thing that worries me most...*now*," she added with a quick glare at me, "is that whatever happened at the lab was bad enough they thought it was worth murdering Cassidy over when they realized she'd collected the data that would reveal their error."

"Did they tell you where her equipment is?" Pete asked. "Any film footage from the drone?"

Sheriff Marge shook her head. "Truitt says Herren destroyed it. Herren says there never was any. If they don't cooperate, we're going to have to seize everything in that lab and sort through the data until we find whatever the secret is." She heaved a sigh. "And we're not scientists. It could take months—we'd have to call in outside experts. *Expensive* outside experts."

Owen had joined our group, a couple small butterfly bandages on his chin and left hand, covering the cuts he'd received from the flying glass when he'd smashed the door. He looked older, wearier, all of a sudden, and it struck me how much of Sheriff Marge's demeanor had rubbed off on him. I didn't know where he'd been, just that he'd been gone for a few days and out of the rotation of our protective detail.

He hitched a thumb into the front pocket of his jeans and said, "The staff at the lab will help, I'm pretty sure of it. Truitt and Herren weren't managing the lab in a way that promoted morale. People will talk."

"In that case," Sheriff Marge reached up to clap him on the shoulder, "come along. We'll have another go at them in the interview room. You should take the lead this time."

~oOo~

It took a week, but Sheriff Marge and Owen got the corroboration they needed to piece together the motive behind Gordon Truitt's and Russ Herren's brutality.

The receptionist at Truitt BotoTechnologies was a font of information, especially when Owen, in all his handsomeness, turned up to interview her in person. She'd known Cassidy, just at a passing acquaintance level, had seen her around the facilities a couple times wearing a visitor's pass, and had known of her research project and her love for the outdoors and for backwoods hiking. It hadn't seemed at all unusual to her that Cassidy would agree to join the two head scientists for a weekend's adventuring. But that had been weeks before anyone realized Cassidy was missing—she hadn't correlated the disparate events until Owen started asking pointed questions.

Russ Herren had stolen the pickup for that subterfuge, and both men had groomed Cassidy into believing they were all heading out to a base camp to meet up with a small group of hikers and a guide.

But, obviously, they'd driven her deep into the forest instead, to a spot they deemed appropriate for dumping her body, keeping up the charade until they'd reached their destination so there would be no blood or signs of a struggle left inside the vehicle should it ever be found after they ditched it.

Sheriff Marge was resting with her hip against the counter in the Imogene's kitchen as she filled me in, looking for all the world like her usual, stoutly healthy self with only the one new anomaly of an herbal tea bag tag dangling from the large insulated travel mug she held. Starched khaki suited her.

Burke was at his first day of school, and I had the closed-on-Monday museum to myself. I was putting the finishing touches on the new exhibit and had invited Sheriff Marge to have the opportunity for an honorary walk-through before it opened to the public.

"And the seed swap, what happened?" I asked.

"The point of no return was actually two summers ago, when Russ Herren accidentally sent the genetic details for the wrong seed strain to SeedGenix—one that hadn't yet received U.S. Food & Drug Administration approval and that the lab was engineering for a different seed company. SeedGenix developed it into a seed crop last year, and that's what they sold to all the region's farmers this summer. One mix-up in the lab, and we now have millions of acres planted with a wheat strain that no one's actually tested in the real world yet."

"Except, they are now, by default," I murmured.

"Exactly. And that's what Cassidy found. A crop that's performing abnormally well. Insane growth rates, even through the winter months. No seed head formation yet, so the jury's still out on production levels. Her data made Russ Herren go back and check his records, and that's when they realized their mistake."

"Truitt knew about it?"

"After the fact, but yes. Impossible for him not to know about it. But he found out in time to limit the damage—from his perspective. He was hoping to eliminate the source of the revealing information, and therefore the information itself. Better to let the farmers think they were just having a bumper year for reasons that had nothing to do with this particular form of genetic development."

"And save his own professional hide."

Sheriff Marge nodded. "That too. The scale of these operations magnifies mistakes. He would've been—is— utterly ruined, professionally, financially. He would've lost everything. But in killing Cassidy, he turned a relatively honest mistake into something even more devastating for himself, and for Herren." Sheriff Marge twirled the tea tag between her thick fingers. "Cover-ups never work, not in the long run."

But my mind was stuck on the closely intertwined economy of the region. "The farmers have all planted a crop they can't sell. This is going to ruin everyone." I could barely squeeze out the words. The breadth of this coming catastrophe was overwhelming.

Sheriff Marge tipped her head, her brow furrowed. "I doubt it. The FDA is holding a series of emergency meetings. They'll approve this strain, no question about it. They have to. Seed technology is one of the industries that's too big to fail, too deeply integrated into the fabric of our national economy. So they'll approve it quietly, and hopefully by harvest no one will remember the questionable origin of nearly thirty percent of the nation's wheat crop. If they do it soon, exports will most likely carry on as normal."

"Is there anything really wrong with this new unapproved wheat strain? Maybe it's safe?" I suggested hopefully. We'd all be eating the breads and cereals and prepackaged goods made from it come next winter, so I surely hoped so.

But Sheriff Marge just shrugged, in a weary sign of resignation. "Honestly? Probably no more or less than any other wheat currently growing in this country." She swept off her hat, revealing her short, salt-and-pepper tufted thatch of hair. "Give me some good news," she said. "How's Burke?"

"Nervous as all get out this morning. Hardly ate anything, so I packed him an extra big lunch. But I think he's excited about school, too." I grinned at the memory of him dashing through his new list of chores, which included feeding Tuppence and sweeping out the mud room on the back porch, his stubbly hair parted neatly and his mineral-green eyes huge as always. He'd been wearing the new clothes he and I had picked out—ones that fit him properly. "Just, you know, the jitters. He hasn't been with kids his own age in several years."

"You should frame that flattened cardboard you and Burke escaped on." Sheriff Marge clucked and shook her head. "Ingenious. Tell that kid I want him to be a deputy when he grows up."

"Too late—about the cardboard, not the kid." I chuckled. "Pete already used the cardboard as a backdrop when he spray-painted a wooden chair to match Burke's desk."

"Settling in, is he?"

"I think so," I noted hopefully. "He needed a quiet place where he could do his homework. I want him to feel like that bedroom is all his, a place where he's safe, where he can think and read and daydream. Where he can be a kid again."

"I meant Pete." Sheriff Marge was giving me an appraising glare over the top of her reading glasses.

"Settling in?" I repeated, thoroughly confused.

"To the idea of fatherhood."

"Oh." I flapped a hand dismissively. "That was never an issue." Definitely not. Pete has a far better handle on what parenting really looks like on a daily basis than I do.

"Good. Then you two can get to work on making a baby sister for Burke."

I blinked. And then scowled at her. Burke's offhand, second-rate suggestion had been spoken in the close confines of our kitchen at home. *Not* public knowledge.

But meddling is the sheriff's—and every other county resident's—natural pastime, and she just leveled that gray gaze back at me with a gleeful smirk and answered—sort of—my unspoken question. "I have my sources."

WHAT'S NEXT?

One of the great delights in writing is the chance to play with story elements: characters, settings, structure, point of view. This new Sockeye County series will give me the chance to expand on the cast of characters from the Imogene Museum series, develop them in more depth in the context of their community and give you a peek inside the heads of many of them.

But there's still definitely a mystery, and I'm having loads of fun incorporating actual local news stories (fictionalized, of course) into the plot. Crazy things that only (but really, truly) happen in the country...

SOCKEYE COUNTY SHORTS
Sockeye County Mysteries #1

Sheriff Marge Stettler has had a county full of misdemeanor vandalism and petty theft for several months now, and the situation is just about to drive her batty. Because it's not normal. In fact, it's almost like someone is orchestrating this spate of stupid criminality—on purpose, just to inflict targeted harm and irritate her.

Or distract her. Because old Griffin Hughes just died, and his auto salvage yard (otherwise known as a collectors' paradise) is being turned into the auction event of the year—in a county that doesn't normally see this kind of action in a collective decade. Or this number of visitors.

So maybe this whole thing is a foil. But for what? And how long do Sheriff Marge and her slender crew of deputies, including the new undersheriff, Ruby Falcone, have to figure it out?

In a sleepy county where everybody knows everybody, someone is sneaking around the edges and rapidly escalating his own nefarious agenda.

NOTES & ACKNOWLEDGMENTS

I'm a firm believer that all good stories are both mysteries and romances at their core. There's always a question that needs to be answered (mystery), and there are always relationships that are integral to the plot (romance, although not always of the two-consenting-adults variety—maybe this concept is better classified as *love*, or even *conflict*...and often both at the same time).

Sometimes, however, I think the most important romance occurs between the reader and the characters on the pages. I know I have that relationship with all my favorite books.

So I've wanted to write another Imogene Museum mystery for a long time, mainly because I also believe that happily-ever-afters aren't wrapped up and tied with a guaranteed bow at the wedding. They take a lot of hard work and faith, but the good knots should go on for the next forty or sixty or eighty years in spite of mysteries and conflict and travails. (Shout out to my parents right here—they're rapidly advancing on the big 50 themselves. We've been threatening them with a monster bash. They are not amused. Did I mention I might've been part of those *travails* as a youngster? Also as an oldster?)

Thanks again, as always, to Debra Biaggi who toted this manuscript around with her through a very busy life in order to read it and provide invaluable feedback. She also tells me funny stories. I think I both laugh and cry in her presence (for only the best reasons) more than I do with any other person. What a treasure.

Also again, as always, I claim all errors, whether accidental or intentional, solely as my own. You may have noticed I did some more, rather extensive, scootching around of geography again, since the pursuit of justice generally requires travel out here in the wild lands of eastern Washington and eastern Oregon, but a lot of that travel is across high-plateau flat stuff that would bore you if it took more than a paragraph or so in the text. (Far, far better if you have the opportunity to see that magnificent expanse in person!)

Deepest gratitude to *everyone* who reads my books—but most especially to those readers who take the time to post reviews online. Your comments continue to make a world of difference, not just for me as an author, but also for all the other readers out there who are considering what new mystery series to dive into. Let the romance begin!

I also have a monthly newsletter in which I share about writing progress, ask for reader input, run the occasional contest or giveaway, and just generally enthuse about books. If that sounds like your cup of tea, you can sign up at my website: jerushajones.com

ABOUT THE AUTHOR

Jerusha writes cozy mystery series which are set along the rivers and amid the forests of her beloved Pacific Northwest. She spends most of her time seated in front of her attic window, engaged in daydreaming with intermittent typing or pinning Post-It notes to corkboards (better safe than sorry!). She also considers maple-frosted, cream-filled doughnuts an essential component of her writer's toolkit.

She posts updates on her website: jerushajones.com

If you'd like to be notified about new book releases, please sign up for her email newsletter on her website. Your email address will never be shared, swapped, or sold and you can unsubscribe at any time.

She loves hearing from readers via email at jerusha@jerushajones.com

ALSO BY JERUSHA JONES

Tin Can Mystery Series
Mercury Rising
Silicon Waning
Carbon Dating
Silver Lining
Lead Flying
Oxygen Burning
Iron Sinking
Neon Warning

Mayfield Mystery Series
Bait & Switch
Grab & Go
Hide & Find
Cash & Carry
Tried & True

Jericho McElroy Mystery Series
The Double-Barreled Glitch

Imogene Museum Mystery Series
Rock Bottom
Doubled Up
Sight Shot
Tin Foil
Faux Reel
Shift Burn
Stray Narrow

Sockeye County Mystery Series
Sockeye County Shorts
Sockeye County Briefs
Sockeye County Au Naturel
Sockeye County Skinny